D0422342

Home Before Dark

Home Before Dark

SUE ELLEN BRIDGERS

a novel

ALFRED A. KNOPF ~~~~~ NEW YORK

For William Woods College Library —

Happy Reading!

Sue Ellen Bridgers

WILLIAM WOODS COLLEGE LIBRARY
57914

This is a Borzoi book published by Alfred A. Knopf, Inc. Copyright © 1976 by Sue Ellen Bridgers. All rights reserved under International and Pan-American Copyright Conventions. Published in the United States by Alfred A. Knopf, Inc., New York, and simultaneously in Canada by Random House of Canada Limited, Toronto. Distributed by Random House, Inc., New York. Library of Congress Cataloging in Publication Data. Bridgers, Sue Ellen. Home before dark. Summary: Returning with her migrant family to her father's childhood home, a fourteen-year-old struggles with her new stationary life. [1. Family life— Fiction 2. Migrant labor—Fiction]. I. Title. PZ7.B7615Ho [Fic] 76-8661 ISBN 0-394-83299-X Manufactured in the United States of America. 10 9 8 7 6 5 4 3 2 1

EMC
PZ
7
B7615
Ho

WILLIAM WOODS COLLEGE LIBRARY
57914

For my mother, Bett

Home Before Dark

Chapter One

The dusty white station wagon turned off the highway onto a narrow asphalt road that shimmered with steam and sunlight, then lurched at the downshift and, sucking air under its belly, roared into third.

In the back seat, Stella pressed her sticky palms against the lumpy, ragged cushion and tried not to sway into the territory claimed by her brother William who dozed next to her. She strained her neck forward to see where their daddy was taking them.

"Hold on," he said, too late. The baby, Lissy, had already slid off her pallett in the luggage space into the narrow corridor of hard, hot floor at four-year-old Earl's feet, and she wailed her baby cries over their daddy's warning.

"Hush up," their mother, Mae, said from the front seat. To Stella, she seemed propped up against her will between the door and a bundle of household goods that separated her from her husband. The wind from the open window caught her butchered, unkempt hair and parted it neatly as she turned wearily to stretch over the back of the seat.

Lissy had already stopped crying and was playing with Earl's feet. The baby pushed her wet fingers between Earl's toes, and he giggled, writhing against the hot window but trying to keep his feet within her reach.

"Stop that, Lissy," Mae said halfheartedly and turned back to the front. "Earl, you get outa her way."

"Earl likes it, and at the same time he don't." Stella answered. "Anyway, there's nowhere else for him to go."

At fourteen, Stella was thin and fair, with the dingy, fading pallor of intermittent sunburns to her skin. She looked like a discarded doll, with dry fibre hair, that had been endowed with human eyelids which were puffy and red from hours of restless sleep in the car. Now she leaned over the back seat and lifted Lissy to pull her into her lap. The baby's hair fell in damp, sticky strings across her cheeks, and Stella pushed them back gently with her hand. She loved the plump, responsive body of the baby, who seemed to want cuddling even in the heat.

"She's so hot," Stella whined softly. "We're all so hot."

"Another couple of miles," James Earl said. "Mae, can you clean 'em up a little?"

"With what?" Mae asked irritably. "My mouth's too dry to make spit." She rummaged through an old straw bag that she kept stashed under her feet and came up with a folded handkerchief. "Here," she said to Stella. "Do what you can."

Stella spit into the handkerchief and held Lissy's thick red cheeks with her hand while she wiped the baby's forehead and mouth. Then she sat the baby down on the seat between herself and the silent William and went after Earl, who scooted against the stacked boxes and bags in the luggage space.

"My face ain't dirty," he said, holding out his hands to her in defense. Stella rubbed them hard with the sticky cloth.

"Your face is too dirty to bother with," she said emphatically, growing excited at having even this tiny chore to do after so many miles of nothing. She handed the cloth to William, and he spit into it and wiped his mouth and cheeks.

"Lord knows, you're all a sight," Stella said to them, including her parents in her verdict.

"Look," James Earl said. They were passing the town sign, and they all leaned toward the right to look at it.

The town eased up on them, one house at a time, until suddenly, almost without warning they felt, they were at its center and James Earl was pulling out of the empty traffic lane and into the red-tiled shelter of a gray stucco service station.

The other children scrambled around inside the rusted station wagon while Stella pushed against the door, which finally screeched open. The children dropped out, one after another, onto the greasy concrete.

"Anybody needs to go, now's the time," James Earl said, heading toward the station where a man stood staring out at them.

"Tell 'em I'll pump it, Daddy," Stella called, already twisting off the gasoline cap.

"It's my turn," William yelled, racing for the pump.

"You take Earl to the bathroom. It's Stella's turn," James Earl said and watched while she rescued the pump from William, stuck the nozzle in, and pushed the lever. While the numbers whirled past, James Earl went on into the station, bought five soft drinks and rummaged through the candy cartons, picking four different kinds of candy and then crackers for Mae and a bag of peanuts that he poured into his own Pepsi bottle. He brought the candy and drinks to the car and, having delivered breakfast, went back into the air-conditioned office and leaned against the slanted glass case, looking out the window at his wife and children.

Mae leaned against the station wagon drinking her soft drink. Holding Lissy in one arm, she lifted the bottle to the baby's mouth and poured the cola in. The child writhed in her arms, and the cola spewed down her chin and clothes. Mae didn't seem to notice but went on drinking, her thin neck moving rhythmically as she swallowed. The children were eating, too, their jaws working resolutely as if the candy were the only thing they had to think about. James Earl knew that at times eating was the only thing that mattered to them. That and sleep.

"Where you headed?" the station attendant asked while counting out James Earl's change.

"This is it," James Earl said almost shyly. "Been living in Florida, all over Florida if you're wanting the truth, for the past sixteen years. Name's Willis. James Earl Willis."

"By God, you're Newton's brother," the man said excitedly. "You headed out to the farm?"

"Yeah," James Earl said. "I'm on my way home."

The land itself was home to him. James Earl, who remembered from sixteen years ago what was planted where and who planted it, drove slowly. The smaller children sat quietly in the back, not knowing they were almost there. They had ridden for a long time, for years it seemed, in the car, and they just knew they'd never get there.

Stella sat up straight in the back seat, looking at everything. She had never heard much about this place they were going to, her daddy's home. Having never had a home herself, she was always surprised when he'd begin remembering aloud something from his childhood. But just when she was really interested and ready to question him more, he stopped himself short, as if he didn't want to spur on her curiosity.

"Lord, it was so long ago," he would say. "I don't remember, Stella." But he'd say it looking at Mae instead of her. It was her mother that didn't want him to remember, who didn't want to hear.

"How much longer is it, Daddy?" Stella asked softly.

"Just a couple of miles," James Earl said. "I used to walk this road into town. Your great-granddaddy owned a lot of this land once, but by the time I came along he'd lost most of it. We had enough to make a good living, though."

Stella caught the growing excitement in his voice. "Did you live in the same house all the time, Daddy?" she asked, almost afraid to imagine something so remarkable as that about him.

"Sure I did, honey. The same house my daddy grew up in. We had it modernized, of course. I remember helping your granddaddy put in the hot-water heater when I was a lot younger than you. That very night, Mama ran a washtub of hot water, and I took a bath in the kitchen. I can remember the look on Mama's face to this day. She was just beaming, with that steam coming up around the spigot and into her face."

"And you had a room with a fireplace in it, didn't you?" Stella asked, trying to remember all the scattered bits of his life she'd stored away.

"Yeah. Almost every room had a fireplace, but we didn't light the bedroom fires except when we were sick. We stayed in the parlor or in the kitchen in the winter time. When Mama sent me up to bed, I can tell you I went in a hurry. You don't mess around in that kind of cold. The bed would be icy and my teeth would be chattering—you've never felt anything like it, Stella."

"I'd like to, though," she said.

"A house brings things with it, that's a fact," James Earl said. "But somehow I've forgotten most of the everyday things and just remember what was special to me. Like that bath I remember taking. I guess I washed in that kitchen hundreds of times before we got plumbing all over the house, but I remember that first time when we got running hot water because it was real special." He gave Stella a glancing smile. "It used to be a fine house, Stella."

"I wish I had a house to stay in," she started.

"Hush up," Mae said suddenly, and Stella knew to be quiet. She leaned back against the seat and shut her eyes to study the house she was imagining.

"When we get there, I'll go in first," James Earl was saying to Mae. "You and the kids just stay in the car. We can't all go in right off."

"I know," Mae said without understanding. She didn't know James Earl except as her husband.

"Newton's probably married by now. After all, he's twenty-six years old." James Earl paused a moment and watched the road intently, as if he envisioned his brother in the steamy air before him.

He looked at Mae again, but she was looking at

the fields. The thick green, leafy tobacco plants seemed foreign to her. It was a dry, dusty jungle without the sweet citrus smell or the low open space of bean fields that meant home to her. He'll stay forever, she realized with sudden clarity, or he won't stay at all.

They came upon a thick wood, and the trees, heavy with summer, darkened the car and diluted the hot wind that blew in on them. Suddenly the woods cleared and sunlight made them blink.

"Here it is," James Earl said, stopping the car.

Mae looked at him. The house and the brother didn't matter. All that counted for her was in the station wagon, was next to her gripping the wheel and looking tearful. She hadn't expected to see him weakened by love so soon.

"Look at it," James Earl said sharply, and she turned abruptly toward the window.

The house was big and white, with a deep front porch and tall narrow windows. It looked like what it was—the old homeplace made modern by succeeding generations. The front had been extended past the porch on both sides, and the extensions were of old brick with small square windows and shutters. The original clapboard was now aluminum siding.

"Is this it?" Stella asked, leaning forward between her parents. "Oh, Daddy, it's so beautiful. It's just like I knew it would be."

The boys began pushing to get out.

"Wait," Mae said angrily. "Sit still." Her command seemed as unreasonable to her as it did to them.

"I'll be back in a minute." James Earl slipped out of the car and shut the door.

Mae felt the hot breeze on her arms and face. She wanted to cry, trapped as she was in the car. Instead,

Chapter Two

James Earl's brother, Newton, let them move into an empty tenant house at the end of a lane that ran beside the homeplace back into the farmland.

"It's not much," Newton said during dinner that noon. He seemed unable to hide his surprise at seeing the faces crowding his table, and so his face was contorted between smiles and worried looks of important decision making. "We put a bathroom in it a few years back, but with help so short nobody's lived there in over a year now."

"It'll be all right, Newt," James Earl said. "You've done fine with the whole place, and I know I'm not bringing anything to this arrangement but two hands and a back." He looked at his children, who ate quickly and silently. Around this table, they looked like liabilities to him. His eyes settled on Stella. "Stella likes to work. Don't you, honey?"

She stared up at him, her fork in midair. She was being called on to perform in public for the first time other than in truck-stop restaurants, where they sometimes got a chance to have the lunchtime special and she was appointed to negotiate for extra packets of catsup and sugar. She had a flair for these public dramatics, having played the role first as a chubby, blond toddler to whom nothing could be denied. She had had a honey-rich blush about her then, and as she had grown older, becoming thin, almost frail, she had learned that plaintive eyes and a pouting mouth could be as profitable as a cherubic face. Perhaps the waitresses, thin and plaintive themselves, saw the determination of her eyes, the melodramatic twist of her lip, and thought to themselves, what's ten cents worth of catsup if it helps this kid make it?

But now Stella hesitated, wondering what the unpracticed answer could possibly be. "I like picking," she said finally. "I like picking oranges and peaches too, because they smell good."

Everybody sighed and went back to eating while Anne, Newton's wife, refilled the serving dishes. "Have some more," she kept saying. They looked half-starved to her.

Mae seemed ill-at-ease, she thought, painfully incapable of anything but embarrassment. The younger children, with their stares and scrawny bodies, looked like mouth-moving statues, little ventriloquist dummies at her table. Only Stella seemed to have a spark.

Anne, holding a woven breadbasket laden with hot biscuits, stopped at the girl's chair and passed the basket over her shoulder, touching Stella gently with the back of her hand as she put the biscuits on the table. Stella didn't move away, and so Anne rested her hand a moment, until Stella turned quickly and gave her a little smile.

"Good biscuits," she said. "Aren't they good biscuits, Daddy?" She turned back to the table. It seemed important that she and James Earl prove themselves.

"Good as Mama ever made," James Earl said, "and that's saying something."

"Mama don't make no biscuits," William said solemnly. They sounded like the first words out of a ten-year-old's mouth.

"Not your mama," James Earl laughed. "My mama."

They were silent—James Earl, Newton, Anne—conjuring up the memory of the mother in the kitchen, at the table, kneading, serving, blessing. In the silence, the others struggled to catch the mystery of the woman's presence and absence, but imagination failed them and they went back to eating.

"As soon as you get settled in the house, we'll make some biscuits, Mae," Anne said.

"I thank you," Mae said softly without looking up from her plate. There was no one she could look at.

Since the house wasn't furnished, Newt went into the attic where he and Anne had stored some of the old family furniture and came up with a kitchen set, a sofa and two beds, an extra mattress, and the crib James Earl and Newton had slept in. James Earl recognized the extra mattress although it had big brown stains covering the quilted yellow roses on one side.

"That was Mama's," he said. "I remember it was the first mattress I ever saw that wasn't plain ticking. What the hell is that?"

"She bled on it," Newt said, turning the mattress against the wall so he could get to some kitchen chairs.

The attic was unbearably hot. Stifling dust hung like hot smoke in the air. James Earl could hear the children playing in the yard below. He turned away from the mattress and supported himself with his hands on the jamb of the open window. The children were playing red rover on the bright carpet of grass, and someone had caught Baby Earl hard in the gullet. He sat on the grass holding his throat and screaming.

"I guess I thought she just died," James Earl said slowly. "You know, without any pain or anything."

"She killed herself," Newton answered. He paused as if expecting James Earl to turn to him, but the man still leaned against the window, looking down at his children.

"She had cancer," Newton said more gently. "But I guess she knew she could live like that a long time. Anne was here that day. She found her. Mama had been sitting up, propped against the pillows, and she held a revolver I'd given her six or seven years before right against her stomach under the blanket."

Outside, Mae had gone to Baby Earl and was holding him. He had stopped crying, but still she sat on the ground, the child in her arms, rocking him. Her thin back swaying from the hips, she comforted herself.

"I thought she just died," James Earl whispered. The words seemed so absurdly childish that he wanted to snatch them back.

"We didn't know where you were, so I wrote letters to general delivery at the places on the cards you sent Mama. She kept them in a box on her dresser."

"I got it in Orlando a month or so later. Too late." James Earl breathed in the fresh air from the attic window. The children were playing again and Mae had disappeared.

"How about this table?" Newt asked, wiping dust

off it with a dirty rag. "You know, James Earl, what I really regret is that I didn't understand what Mama was going through. But then, maybe we don't understand any suffering but our own. Mama and I got to where we didn't talk very much; so when the time came, I don't reckon she could tell me how bad it was. I couldn't have listened either, or said the right things if I had. I learned something from it, though. That's why I want to be open with you right now."

"We had some good times, didn't we, Newt?" James Earl sat down on a chair and looked at his brother.

"I guess we did. I thought you were the greatest thing on two feet." Newton grinned.

He had a familiar, almost childishly shy expression on his fleshy face, and for a moment he looked like James Earl's memory of him—roly-poly, laughing, what he'd once thought of as "pukey cute."

"I don't remember much now, though," Newt continued, his features turning abruptly into a more masculine face, still fleshy but strongly-defined and almost handsome. "I could always see where I stood in the family. It wasn't just being the youngest. It was being so different from you. You could always do everything better than I could.

"I was glad when you quit school and joined the Air Force. I thought, 'Now it's my turn,' and I worked hard in school and here on the place. Daddy lived to see me make money farming. It's mine, you know, except for those acres on the far side of the pasture. They belonged to Mama outright, and she willed them to you. The rest—the house, everything else—Daddy left to Mama for her lifetime and then to me."

"Seems fair."

Newton looked at him closely. James Earl's face was narrow and painfully drawn, like a sketch made with a charcoal stub. His forehead was long and narrow; his nose too short and flared; his jawline weakening. His face seemed to have slipped a little, missing the mark of youth he'd once had. He needed a haircut, too. Rusty curls looped into his ears and fell down onto his shirt collar.

"Looks like a damn hippie," Newt had said to Anne earlier that afternoon, and she'd smiled and kissed him gently, urging him with her fingers on his shoulders to relax and take strength from her.

"It'll be all right," she had said, and he'd believed her because at the time it was the easiest thing to do.

Now things were different. There was no comforting Anne. Only a gaunt, disturbingly old but ungrown brother across the stifling attic from him. "I just want you to understand. I—we're—glad you've come. Help is scarce and I need you to get the crop in, but I want you to know where you stand."

"I didn't come expecting anything," James Earl said softly. "I just needed to be here, to show Mae and the kids, to see for myself." He brushed his hand across his disheveled hair. "Can you cut hair?" he asked. "I hate like hell to go to town like this."

"I've got some pruning shears," Newton laughed. He felt suddenly happy. "Now let's start hauling this stuff down. We can get most of it over to the house before supper." He stood amidst the clutter, his hands on his hips, his shirt darkened with dirt and sweat, and said, "You want that mattress? We can cover it up with something."

"Don't need to do that. We might as well face hard truths now as later," James Earl said. "Besides, Stella's never seen a mattress with flowers on it."

The house was only half-painted. Coming down the path, Mae and Stella saw the painted half first, and Mae's heart thumped. Suddenly, without thinking, she took Stella's swinging hand. Stella was no more accustomed to being touched than her mother was to touching, and her impulse was to pull away and explore a kind of bursting freedom she felt in her own body.

She can't hold me back anymore, Stella thought, feeling the pressure of Mae's hand on hers. This is the last time she'll tell me to be still or quiet or patient. There won't be any stuffy old car to sit in half the day, while houses go by and I'm wondering what it's like to be living somewhere, anywhere, where I can get to know people who aren't leaving tomorrow.

The house was before them, a shotgun house with a kitchen attached to the back of the side porch and a narrow, low porch on the front. This is where I'm going to live, Stella thought, and let her hand rest in her mother's.

Mae walked slowly and Stella stayed back with her, although she wanted to run and jump on the porch, look into the window, push open the door, and step inside. It's her house, too, Stella thought. It's the best house I can remember, probably the best house she's ever had.

Mae tightened her hand around Stella's thin fingers. "I know it's a handout," she said softly, "but it's all right, ain't it, Stella?"

"Sure it is," Stella said. "We can do lots of things to it. Anne's got magazines about what to do in houses to make them nice. I saw some of them. Pretty rooms with books and statues and wallpaper, like Anne has."

"We can't do none of that," Mae snapped.

I can, Stella thought angrily. I can do anything now and your saying no doesn't matter at all.

They reached the porch and stood in front of it looking at the one side still gleaming in its coat of paint and the other side, defeated, weather-beaten brown. It looked like a half-made-up face.

"We can get some more paint. I bet I can paint it right by myself," Stella said, hardly surprised at the house's double nature.

"We can't do nothing like that. Newton'll have to get it done if it gets done. It's his house. You remember that, Stella. Everything you can see belongs to your daddy's brother." Looking at the house had taken the life out of her, and she released Stella's hand slowly as if she'd died standing there.

"You coming in?" Stella wiped her damp hand on her shorts. She felt clammy with excitement and couldn't help hoping that her mother would let her explore the house alone, free from the doubts that always seemed to color Mae's thinking.

"You go ahead." Mae sat on the porch with her face and shoulders out of the sun. "Well, go on," she said when Stella hesitated. "Go on."

The door swung open without a creak and Stella stepped inside. Because the room was bare, it seemed very large to her. In her mind, it was an empty, dusty world of filtered light waiting for her to clean it up and fill it with her whole life. She walked slowly into the next room and then the next, through shades of brown and gray and sun-bright white, down the narrow side porch into the kitchen and tiny bathroom. Then she turned and, looking back at where she'd been, saw how good living there could be.

She had been born a squalling knot of tight, unexplainable longings that screamed "I will be" to a world that seemed to ignore her, that gave her no safety but the battered shell of an automobile and an armrest on which to pound her silent anger. Now she had a place to store the secret Stella and draw her longings out slowly, carefully, one by one, and keep them safe. She would never desert this place, never let it slip away as her daddy had. They could all vanish, and she would stay, because already what counted for her was here, inside walls that didn't move in the dark or carry her somewhere as strange and unwelcoming as the last place she'd been.

"Stella Mae!"

"Back here," she called and came up the side porch into the bedroom. Her mother stood in the middle room, her hands over her face as if she were afraid to look.

"We can make it real nice, Mama," Stella said. "Come on and look. The kitchen has spigots, and there's a little bathroom with a showerbath in it. It's real nice."

Mae moved her hands and looked at the empty room. Her face was stricken. For a moment contorted with what seemed to be physical pain. Then, a blank.

"We're going to stay, aren't we, Mama? Can't we stay forever and ever?" Stella begged, knowing the answer but wanting it out in the open, clearly visible, where she could fight it better.

"There ain't no forever," Mae said. "We keep moving 'cause that's what we can do."

"Not me," Stella said, filling the little house with her voice until the dust seemed to stir and the thin windowpanes vibrate. "I'm never leaving."

Mae stood in the middle of the handout house and let loose the tears saved up across Georgia and South Carolina, held back in the stinking, oily heat of the station wagon and in the gardenia-scented, air-conditioned space of Anne Willis' living room. Spilling down her trembling cheeks and chin, they said what she could never have found words to say, for she knew that what was a beginning for her child was a final, desperate failure for herself.

James Earl went to work in the fields, priming tobacco next to the tenants until his shoulders ached so painfully that he couldn't straighten up.

"Them sand lugs is the worst, and the worst is always first," Silas said, seeing James Earl squatting in the next row, his face hidden behind the sticky foliage of the tobacco plants. Silas was grinning. He always grinned, even when he was serious, as though his face didn't know what his head was doing. It gave him a stupid, lively look that he knew made people feel good.

James Earl grinned back. He'd known Silas when they were boys and coming home had been as much coming home to people like Silas as to anything. The house, the land, the tenants who farmed it, the very air he breathed was home to James Earl. He raised his shoulders slowly, trying to find a position that didn't hurt.

"Tomorrow you gonna die out here," Silas said. "Sure as the sun comes up, these here lugs gonna kill you."

"You'll be sore, too, Silas. You ain't been bent double lately either, have you?" James Earl wiped his sweaty face with his sleeve, being careful to keep his eyes closed against the bitter tobacco gum.

"Sure I will, but you're the one resting. I just stopped to keep you company. Tell you what, I'll send Toby down to the house tonight with some of Synora's salve. You rub it in good and it'll take the fire right out. Out of everything, if you want to know the truth. But tonight you ain't gonna care about that, are you?"

"Tonight I ain't moving a muscle," James Earl said. "Maybe I ain't moving for a week."

Silas laughed, his chuckle rising slowly until it ripped his mouth and showed even, yellow teeth. He bent down. "Here I go," he said, laughter riding on his voice. "You better come on, too, if you expect them wages."

Wages, James Earl thought, leaning forward to pull a damp, heavy leaf out of the dirt. In his mind the leaf lost weight, burned brittle golden, bright-leafed and sweet smelling. The wages were nothing for a man thirty-two years old. Tobacco prices weren't what they used to be, either.

It's like I've been moving and standing still all these years, he thought. But now I'm home, and that counts for something. Tenant wages or not, I'd rather be in this dirt than anywhere else I've been.

"James Earl!" It was Silas halfway down the row. "Your ass stuck?"

"I'm coming."

"It's time to eat." Silas dropped his leaves into the narrow burlap-sided cart and yelled up the land to his son, Toby. "Come get this mule outa here!"

Toby, slick with sweat, his dark hair dripping on his forehead, puffed up the dusty road to the mule and truck. "Dinnertime, Daddy," he said, jumping onto the back of the truck. He took the reins and clucked to the mule.

"You ain't tellin' me nothin' I don't already know, boy. My stomach tells me when it's dinnertime." Silas still grinned, but his expression was somehow different, almost shy, as though he were risking his own defenses when he spoke to his only child.

"Toby's what counts for me, James Earl," he said, watching his son's straight, muscular body leaning forward, balancing his bare feet with the rumbling sway of the truck. "I ain't never goin' count for nothin'. What could I be, the president? But Toby. He's got brains."

They walked slowly along in the dust of the truck, the noon sun burning into their aching shoulders like liniment.

So Silas is looking toward the future, James Earl thought. As for himself, he'd never been concerned beyond the next picking station, had never given much thought to what would become of his children. They had always seemed so little to him, so new, that their futures were beyond his imagination. He knew he would have stayed on the road forever were it not for this compulsion to see his home and brother again. He hadn't come for Stella. He could have let her grow up in an automobile, without her ever knowing what roots meant. How could he have lived so completely in the present and not realized that Stella deserved a chance to be somebody as much as Toby did?

He kicked a rock with his foot and watched the dirt leap into the air, tiny particles of earth rising and then settling back beneath his feet. In the distance, he saw a thin, blond figure dart out from under a barn shelter and jump onto the truck next to Toby. The dust was like a curtain between James Earl and his daughter, and at that moment he would have brushed it away if that meant seeing what her life would be like if they stayed or if they went. Stella balanced precariously next to Toby, and James Earl came in slowly behind them, knowing that at least today life was good to her.

Already she had Toby for her first real friend. The day after their arrival, Silas and Synora had come shyly to the back door, Toby behind them, to welcome James Earl home. The first thing James Earl had noticed was how bashful Toby was, hanging in his parents' shadow as though he were less than confident about meeting Stella, who didn't hold shyness among her attributes. She had jumped right off the porch, practically into the poor boy's arms, in her excitement at finding somebody near her own age.

"This is Stella," James Earl remembered saying. "She's been wondering what she was going to do around here."

"I work all day," Toby had said as if that would save him from her.

"Doing what?" Stella asked.

"Trucking tobacco, putting up sticks. Whatever Mr. Newton says to do."

"I guess I'll be doing that, too," Stella said.

"Girls don't truck tobacco. You'd have to drive a mule."

"I can do it if Uncle Newton says I can." Stella plopped down on a patch of grass, while the grown-ups settled on the steps.

"You know how to drive a mule?" Toby asked, still standing.

"No, but you didn't always know how."

Toby must have known he was losing because he changed the subject. "What grade are you at school?"

"The eighth, I guess. Last year I didn't get to go much. Mama stayed sick for the longest time after my baby sister was born. But this year I'm going every single day. What grade are you in?"

"Ninth. High school," Toby said happily. School seemed to be one thing he was confident about.

"Uncle Newton says I can ride the bus. Do you ride the bus?"

"I'm not sitting with a girl, if that's what you're wanting to know."

"I'm just making conversation, Toby Brown, so you won't be standing there like a knot on a stick."

"Stella don't waste time getting acquainted," James Earl had interjected to spare Toby's having to answer.

"Yeah, well, I got to get going," Toby had said, edging away from them all.

"I'll see you in the morning!" Stella called after him. "What time do you start work?"

"By six," Toby said, obviously hoping to discourage her.

"Oh, I'm always up by then," Stella replied.

And of course she was, if for no other reason than that Toby had inadvertently challenged her.

Now James Earl saw them tying the mule under the shelter and racing off toward the house.

"Looks like they'd be tired," he said to Silas.

"Work's still fun to them," Silas said, "and if they're lucky, it always will be. I can't think of nothin' better to spend my time doing."

"But you want something different for Toby," James Earl said.

"Yeah. Something better."

"That's what I want for Stella, too," James Earl said, knowing that it was true.

Chapter Three

Stella, wrapped in a towel, her hair and shoulders glistening with water from the shower, was standing in the middle of the kitchen when Toby knocked on the kitchen door.

"Stella!" he called, pressing his face against the screen. "You in there, Stella?"

"I'm not dressed, Toby," she said, coming close to the door so he could see the towel. "I'm dripping wet. Been standing in that shower fifteen minutes."

"I brought another batch of salve. Mama says you all must be eating the stuff, it goes so fast," Toby smiled. "She's as proud as a peacock, anyhow. None of the Willises ever used her salve before. You planning to let me in?"

"See this towel, Toby? Anne gave it to me. I can wrap these roses around me twice." She turned around in the tiny kitchen to show him. "I'll be back in a minute." She sauntered across the kitchen and into the bathroom.

When she came out on the porch dressed in seersucker shorts and a wrinkled shirt, Toby was sitting on the steps. Stella sat down next to him and began combing her hair. Drops of water flipped off her comb into his face, and Toby shut his eyes and leaned forward to catch the spray on his head.

"You got the cleanest hair in Montreet County," he said. "You're goin' wash it out if you aren't careful."

"That's stupid, Toby. Sometimes you can be just so stupid. Anne's got magazines just for ladies that tell all about hair and skin and pretty clothes. They say you can't wash your hair too much. Besides," she said, smoothing her hair with her hand and striking what she thought was a magazine pose, "just because you don't ever wash yours . . ."

"I'm as clean as you are," Toby said. "I just don't wash unless I'm dirty."

"You're just mouthing off, anyway." Stella jumped up and walked into the yard. "I'm going to paint this house, Toby. You wanna help?"

"I've been trucking tobacco all day and putting up sticks till suppertime and you're asking me if I want to paint a house?" Toby came out and looked at the gray weatherboards with her.

"Newton and Daddy are just too busy. Besides, the best time is late in the day, isn't it?" Stella took his arm and pulled him farther out toward the woods. "Look at it, Toby. We could make it nice. Newton'll buy the paint, and there's brushes already at his house. I've seen them. We could make it nice."

"You got a ladder?" Toby asked reluctantly.

"I can get one."

"You got turp and stirrers?"

"I can get 'em. Please, Toby."

"You gotta pay me," Toby said stubbornly.

"Toby, you're as hateful as a rattlesnake," she said, letting go his arm and stamping off down the road. "I'll paint the goddamn house myself," she yelled into the woods.

"Stella!" Toby stood in the yard still holding the peanut-butter jar of salve. He dropped the jar on the ground and took off after her. "Stella!" The dust stirred around his feet and legs, coating him with gray powder.

"You're getting me dirty," Stella said angrily when he'd caught up. She wouldn't look at him, but marched resolutely on into the woods.

"I'll help you, Stella," Toby said. "Saturday, I'll help you."

She didn't answer, and he saw her cheeks were flushed, suddenly fuller and more soft. Her hair was drying in white wisps around her face.

"I can do it myself," she repeated, refusing to look at him.

Toby gave up and stood in the path while Stella tramped on into the shadows. "Stella," he called when she was almost out of sight, heading nowhere, but away from him. "Please let me paint the house!"

"All right!" the answer came from the woods, and Toby, somehow the victor, went home.

Early Saturday morning they started painting. Toby thought surely they'd get done by afternoon when his daddy and James Earl climbed onto the back of Newton's pickup and went into town. Mae and Toby's mother were up at the house helping Anne slice and sugar peaches to be served up pink and icy from her freezer in winter, and the children played in the yard where William had tied himself to a rusty wagon and was pulling Lissy and Earl around on all fours.

Toby hung onto the ladder and watched the truck disappear down the road, leaving him at the mercy of Stella, who was turning into a tyrant with a personal slave.

"You're missing a place, Toby," she said from the ground, where she'd gone to inspect his work.

"I'm resting," Toby grumbled. "And I ain't missing nothing."

"Well, you are," Stella argued. "I know your intentions are the best, Toby, but you're too close up there to see what you're missing."

"Now I should grow my arms, I reckon, so I can stand down there with you and paint up here," Toby said, slapping paint onto the weatherboards.

"You can't take a bit of criticism, can you, Toby? Not one little bit. Or advice, either." Stella came back to where she'd left her paint can and brush and began painting as high as she could reach below Toby.

He couldn't really complain about her. Stella had painted more than he had. Of course, being on the ladder handicapped him. It was rickety and he had to struggle with his knees to stay balanced. Looking down, he watched her steady, dauntless strokes. She could do anything she set her mind to, and he liked her for it.

"When we get through, let's hitch a ride into town," Toby said to improve his own disposition. "We could get a grape soda and sit around awhile."

Stella looked up, her face red from the heat and splattered with white freckles of paint. "You asking me to town?" she whispered through her teeth.

"Yeah. You got to get that paint offa you first, though," Toby said, continuing to paint as if her almost speechless reaction hadn't flustered him. "I'm not taking you anywhere like that."

"You don't look like much yourself," Stella said gaily. "You've got paint on your head." She painted more quickly. "What else can we do?"

"Well, if you weren't coming, I'd shoot me a little pool, but with you along, I'll just see what's happening, look around in Maggie Grover's Department Store, sit in the soda shop awhile. Nothing much."

"Sounds like a real good time to me," Stella said. "Thanks for asking me, Toby."

The tone in her voice forced Toby to look down. He felt suddenly warmer than the afternoon sun could make him. It was a heat deep inside that told him that maybe he didn't have to go it alone now. It seemed possible that here was someone who could know that he'd read hundreds of books from the school library, and that the librarian borrowed special ones from the high-school library just for him. Perhaps he could tell her that his mind wandered in class because he knew more details of history than the teacher did, that he kept a ledger book of the ideas that came to him hidden in a crevice behind his mother's chiffonier, and that when he read and wrote late into the night in the dark silent house, he imagined that he was Abe Lincoln by firelight.

Here was Stella Willis, a girl as poor as himself but with a family name that had always been respected in the town; a girl with spunk and temper, whom he didn't pretend to understand but nevertheless felt he could risk trusting. He had made her happy, and he felt like crying with joy himself. Instead, he painted quickly, dipping the brush and catching the drips carefully as if painting the house were very important to him.

"We'll be finished in thirty minutes," he said after a while. "You go on and get cleaned up."

"I'm not leaving till it's done," Stella said, stepping back to look at the house again. "You've got to move the ladder one more time."

"I can do it. You go ahead and get cleaned up." Toby climbed down.

"We're doing this together," Stella said, taking his paint can while he moved the ladder a couple of feet toward the corner.

Toby settled the ladder against the house and climbed up quickly, hurrying to get away from her. His heart was suddenly racing and his legs trembled as he tried to fix his knees against the rungs for support.

I'm worn out, he thought. That's what's the matter. But he knew it wasn't. He was trembling because of Stella. She was too close. He could reach down and touch her head, the bright crown of hair she wore. He felt keenly the risk of making a fool of himself. He saw how truly alien she was to him, how little he knew about her. Everything about her seemed a mystery. He could feel himself falling. The ground would be like a sponge to absorb him. He gripped the ladder tenaciously. Not yet, he thought, while the sunlight woozed his brain. Not yet.

Stella wore a dress into town, a light blue, sleeveless one with a white collar and tiny pearl buttons down the front to the waist. Anne had given the dress to her after collecting outgrown clothes from among her friends in town. Stella knew the dress was a hand-me-down, but it looked new and it was the only dress she had.

They got a ride into town with Anne, who was picking up more freezer containers from the grocery store. Stella rode in the front seat of the yellow Buick while Toby, wearing a white T-shirt and pressed, cut-off jeans, sat in the back.

"You take care of her now, Toby," Anne said, looking at him through the rearview mirror. "Take her around a little and introduce her to the young people in the soda shop. I should be doing that myself." She smiled apologetically at Stella. "You tell them she's Newton's niece," she added to Toby.

Toby looked out the window. He was flying, and the fields spinning by blurred into the sky.

How he wanted to drive this car, or at least sit in the front where he could study the leather panel closely and try the radio. Anne never turned on the radio when he hitched a ride with her. She'd complained once of the rock-and-roll music because it was all you could hear anymore, and then she'd acknowledged that Toby probably liked that kind of music. Still she never played the radio, so Toby relied on the soda shop jukebox and someone else's dimes.

Now he watched the back of Stella's head; the fine blond hair like cornsilk, smoothly brushed and lying, although bluntly cut, against her neck. Her neck was slender and lightly browned. He could see the curve behind her ears, where the skin was pink and scrubbed clean.

Stella must feel all the things I feel, he thought suddenly, and wanted to touch her shoulder so she'd turn to him. He had made her happy by inviting her into town for a soft drink. That was all it took.

"I'll let you out here," Anne said, stopping the car in front of a grocery store. "You find Newton and get a ride home tonight," she added. "I don't want Stella down here when it gets dark."

"Yes, ma'am." Toby slipped out of the car in time to open Stella's door.

Stella looked at him with surprise and got out, grinning. "Thanks, Anne," she said. "We'll be all right."

She started down the sidewalk, her dingy white sandals slapping the concrete, and then stopped and turned around, waiting for Toby to join her. She was smiling and bouncing up and down on the balls of her feet, clicking the sandals as if every second wasted were more than she could bear. "Where we going first?" she wanted to know.

"Let's get a drink," Toby said, pushing his hands into his pockets. "And maybe play a song on the jukebox."

"You've got money for the jukebox?" Stella was swinging her skirt as if she intended to start dancing on the sidewalk.

"Maybe one song," Toby said sheepishly.

"Oh, Toby, this is the nicest day. First we got the house looking pretty and now we're downtown right by ourselves going to get a drink in a booth and hear some music. I just can hardly believe it!"

Neither could Toby.

Chapter Four

Rodney Biggers, sixteen on March twelfth and carrying his plastic-coated driver's license between an I Will Not Smoke pledge card and a ten-dollar bill in his wallet, sat at the soda shop counter and stirred his cola with a pink and white plastic straw. The ice was long melted, leaving the drink dark at the bottom and clear on top, but Rodney's stirring wasn't intended to remedy that. He was bored, and watching reddish brown liquid swirling in the paper cup gave him something to do.

He'd already put a quarter in the jukebox and pushed "Fire and Rain" twice. He liked that song, especially the sad way James Taylor sang it. Rodney had heard a girl say right here in the soda shop that the song was about taking drugs. She'd read it in *Time* magazine, so Rodney believed her.

He'd never read *Time* magazine. The only things he ever read that weren't school assignments were the joke pages in the copies of *Reader's Digest* at his mother's beauty shop. He read them to the dull, blowing sound of hairdryers and tried hard to remember the funniest ones, but he wasn't clever that way. Anyhow, he liked "Fire and Rain" no matter what it was really about, because to him it meant feeling low and restless and that was how Rodney felt most of the time.

"You finished with that?" Elsie, the countergirl, asked him, nodding at the warm cola in the crumpled cup. Rodney had peeled the wax coating from under the curled rim, leaving tiny bits of white wax on the counter.

"It ain't fit to drink," Elsie said. She wanted to clean up.

"Well, I'm not finished with it," Rodney said, sweeping the bits of wax into his hand and dropping them into a black plastic ashtray on the counter.

The advertisement written in white letters on the face of the ashtray read "Jean's Beauty Shop—Cut, Curl, Color—Night Appointments." Rodney spun the ashtray and the wax bits spilled onto the words.

Night appointments meant he cooked supper for himself and his daddy. He really liked to cook, so he didn't mind that. His mother wasn't much in the kitchen anyway; the food she prepared ended up smelling like waving lotion or hair spray. The smells about her, the heavy lacquered sheen of her black hair, the dyed tips of her fingers, were the things that consciously annoyed him. They were such unnatural things, these smells and colors, and they embarrassed him.

Right now, his daddy was out on the farm paying off the hands so they could come into town and spend a week's wages in three hours, and his mother stood on aching feet in white, crepe-soled shoes behind the head of some talker.

"That's what the beauty business is all about," his mother liked to say. She didn't just fix the outside of heads, she listened to the inside.

As a philosopher, his mother was matched locally

only by the preacher at the Free Will Baptist Church who liked to say that there wasn't a thing he hadn't heard at least once and nothing at all that had surprised him.

Rodney heard his mother's customers' secrets one by one; she had a way of letting them slip out as if she couldn't remember what was told her in confidence and what wasn't. She ended up telling everything to his daddy, who nodded at her pauses without listening. He'd heard it all before, too.

But from the time he was a little boy, Rodney had found himself listening intently, and he remembered these modern horror tales much as he would have remembered nursery rhymes and fairy tales, had he heard any. He never repeated the stories that spilled off his mother's tongue because he wouldn't be able to tell about family fights or binges or men running around without turning all shades of red and then repenting on his knees afterward, when his conscience would get to him about the sin of gossip, which he knew was a sin no matter what his mother said.

So Rodney kept his mouth shut. But because he saw these people daily and could associate them in his slow-moving mind only with their troubles, he remembered vividly the concrete evidence of sin, and its memory made him as straight and narrow as a new lightning rod. He would never fall into danger because he appreciated the trouble it would bring him. He had put his name on his smoking-pledge card with a black Magic Marker so big it practically covered the printed words. He'd been baptized in the church baptistry, which had certainly washed away any sins he could have accumulated before the age of ten. Since then, he'd known where temptation lurked and avoided it so carefully that he was barely sociable. He intended never to drink, steal, or fornicate, and he protected himself from the sin of unclean thoughts—his own fantasies—by attributing them to what he'd heard rather than to any originality on his own part. Rodney rarely if ever had an original thought—except when he was cooking, where he eagerly substituted rosemary or oregano for bay leaves and concocted his own mayonnaise and barbecue sauce.

Despite his cooking skills and the minimal exercise he got, he'd managed to stay thin through puberty. He scrubbed his face with medicated soap and shaved occasionally, so he always looked clean. His mother could afford to buy him nice clothes and she did, although he refused to wear some of her purchases. She liked flashy colors and wide-legged, cuffed pants. Finally, Rodney had consented to a pair of candy-striped jeans and a red knit shirt which he always wore on Saturday afternoons and then again on Mondays.

When Stella and Toby entered the soda shop, Stella saw Rodney first because she was looking at everything. Toby, who'd seen Rodney in his outfit Saturday after Saturday, didn't even notice him until Stella started tugging at his arm and nodding toward the counter where Rodney sat.

"Who's that?" she whispered.

"It's just Rodney Biggers," Toby muttered, although he was pleased that the first person they'd seen was somebody he knew.

"Let's sit at the counter," Stella said loudly.

"I thought you wanted a booth." Toby pointed toward the nearest one, which was dirty with the remains of two hamburgers and an order of fries in their greasy red and white boat. The red plastic seats were patched with yellow tape, but the batting stuck out around its edges.

"It's dirty," Stella said and sat down next to Rodney Biggers.

The stool had once been a spinner, but now it leaned precariously on its pedestal, and Stella put her arms on the counter to keep from slipping off. Toby sat next to her and ordered two grape sodas from Elsie while Stella looked at Rodney. She stared at him openly, without bothering with sidelong glances, while Rodney studied his fingernails.

"I'll have a grape soda, too," he said to Elsie without looking up. He pushed the messy cup away as though it didn't belong to him.

"Rodney, whatcha' know, buddy?" Toby said, and Rodney found himself forced to look straight at Stella and then past her to Toby.

He grinned too widely. "Nothin' much," he said and thumped the lever on the straw dispenser so heavily that two dropped out.

"This is Stella, Mr. Newton Willis' niece. She just came last week," Toby said.

Stella sipped her soda and then flashed Rodney a smile. "Toby is the nicest person," she said in a strangely sophisticated voice. "This morning he helped me paint our house and now he's brought me to town."

Rodney thought the conversation was already beyond his grasp, and he looked around Stella at Toby.

"Whatcha' know?" he said glumly.

"We're going to look in the stores some, just mess around all afternoon," Stella answered happily. She sipped the soda daintily, "I bet you're in high school."

Rodney puffed up. "Yeah. I'm a sophomore," he said proudly.

"No kidding," Stella said. "And you know Toby? Isn't that something!"

"We were in junior high together two years ago," Toby said. "Rodney's sixteen. He's got wheels."

Rodney felt as if he were watching his own creation.

"No kidding. You've got a car?" Stella bounced on the rickety stool, and Toby grabbed her arm to keep her from falling off.

"It's Mama's," Rodney admitted. "But I've got it today. It's right out front there. A baby blue Impala with V-8 and factory air." He was grinning uncontrollably. Nothing could have pushed his lips back together.

"Where you going in it?" Stella asked.

"I don't know," Rodney said, beginning to deflate. "Nowhere, I reckon." His tight lips relaxed across his teeth.

Most Saturdays he let the car sit down the street at the beauty shop. All week he thought about where he'd go during the weekend, but when Saturday came his plans always seemed not worth the trouble and he just didn't feel like going ahead with them. He often used having to run errands for his mother as an excuse for not doing anything more exciting. He had to keep himself available.

"You could just ride around and look at things," Stella suggested.

"Look at what?" Rodney became more dumb by the minute. Girls generally ignored him so completely that he was totally unprepared for conversation with someone like Stella.

"At anything. At everything!" Stella was exasperated and turned to Toby. "We could go for a ride in Rodney's car with him, couldn't we?"

"I guess so," Toby said slowly. He wanted to ride around and listen to the radio, but the idea frightened him a little. Suddenly, he felt responsible for Stella, whose strong-mindedness seemed likely to override his judgment. Sometimes she seemed to know so little, even less than he did.

"Please, Toby." She was patting his arm anxiously, her blue eyes bluer because of the dress she wore, her fine hair touselling as she bounced on the stool. It came so easy to her, this intimacy with which he had to take such tremendous care. But what could he do?

"You want to show Stella around?" he asked Rodney. "Maybe over to Lawrence and back?"

"I reckon so. You're comin', too, aren't you?" Rodney was scared to death.

Toby sucked the last of his soda up the straw and slid off the stool. "Yeah. I guess I'll come along."

Minutes later, Stella sat in the middle of the front seat strapped in by a seatbelt, because that was one of Jean Biggers' rules. The strap made Stella feel good, more secure than she'd ever felt in the rumbling old station wagon that constantly pitched her against the door. Now she felt cared for, and so she sat up straight with her shoulder touching Toby's, looking prim and detached from the excitement the two boys were trying to hide. The car had sat in the sun for hours, and they became damp and sticky while waiting for the air conditioner to cool them with its clammy breeze.

Finally, cool air hit their legs and faces, and Stella sighed. "This is the nicest day," she said to both of them.

Toby flipped on the radio and Ike and Tina Turner blared out.

"Everybody buckled in?" Rodney asked like a pilot instructing his passengers above the roar of his engines. "Everybody ready?"

He reversed the car in the parking lot and turned slowly out into the traffic.

"Lawrence—15 Miles," read the intersection sign. It was Rodney's longest road trip.

Sitting in the Impala at the Dairy Queen west of Lawrence, Toby knew they'd be too late to find Newton in town and get a ride home.

Out under one of the umbrellas on an aluminum bench, Stella sat licking a chocolate-covered custard that Rodney had bought, while Rodney sat across the table from her watching her careful sideways licks that prevented drips onto her hand. Rodney had ordered himself a cone and had offered one to Toby, but Toby had refused and stayed in the car which had been, for a few minutes, cooler than outside. Now he wished he'd gotten out with them and let Rodney buy him an ice cream, too. If Stella could stand out there in that flimsy old dress and say "Thank you, ma'am" to the lady who pushed the cone out of the cubicle to her, so could he. He could be letting Rodney Biggers pay, too.

Frustrated by his inability to act, Toby watched Rodney finishing his cone. Rodney stuffed the flat end into his mouth as if he were going to swallow the napkin around it, wiped his mouth with the

WILLIAM WOODS COLLEGE LIBRARY

57914

crumpled paper, dropped it on the table, and sat watching Stella, who suddenly pointed to the sky at a low-flying plane.

Toby could see Rodney's mouth moving rapidly. He was learning how to talk to a girl, and Stella was listening intently to the answers to her questions, as she had in the car on their way to Lawrence when Rodney had driven slowly as if he were a tour guide.

Rodney had even explained to her about tobacco warehouses when he didn't know a thing about them, Toby thought. What did he ever do but come to Lawrence the first day the market opened and stand around with a crowd of farmers who paid twenty-five cents for canned soft drinks out of machines because suddenly they expected a good year, a good crop. Money. Rodney just followed his daddy around, looking. Toby had seen him while he, Toby, was unloading graded tobacco from the truck, sweat running into his pants, dripping into his eyes, and his daddy saying, "Hurry up, boy. Gotta get outa here 'fore the bidding starts."

And the bidding; the loud, constant stream of numbers going higher and higher, splitting Toby's head with the roar of money. Oh, he could tell Stella about the warehouse: the concrete floor that always chilled his bare feet no matter how hot the air was, the smell of motor oil and bourbon, the rich, yes rich, smell of tobacco. It burned his nose, seeped into his clothing, put soft dust in his eyes, so that later, at night when he was home again, he could still smell, see, feel it.

There were men there wearing overalls and diamond rings who spat on the floor, men stinking in Big Mac suits, or smelling like the barber shop in spectator shoes and slick dress suits. He'd seen a man once handling a roll of hundred-dollar bills that could have been ones for all the man seemed to care. He waved them in his hand carelessly, and Toby envisioned one, just one, floating down to his own feet and the man saying, "Keep it, son."

Toby could tell her about other times, too. More private moments when he was alone at dawn in the packhouse, with the smell so pure it went straight into his pores, while the birds fluttered loudly under the roof—the only sound; about hanging onto the back of the truck with his head still pressed tight with sleep and one arm pushing gently down on the canvas-covered load, being careful not to crush one precious stem, as if the tobacco meant his life, because it did.

He could tell her how it felt to step on mice and feel the soft infant bodies rolling under his boot until the floor was bloody and raw. Or how the sky looked on nights when he lay in a tobacco truck under the stars, not because Newton needed him to watch the barns but because he wanted the feeling of being completely alone, just Toby Brown and the barn owls and the old cat sleeping at his feet and so many stars the sky seemed on fire.

He could say all that if he and Stella were alone, if they were sitting on the steps of the house they'd painted. He shut his eyes to see the house because it was a visible sign of what he and Stella could do.

"Don't you want anything?" Stella was asking through the window.

"Nope," Toby said lazily. "We better get back, though. Mr. Newton's more than likely already gone home."

"Rodney'll take us, won't you, Rodney?" Stella straightened up and smiled at Rodney over the hood. She already knew she had a way with him, and she climbed into the car without waiting for his answer.

"We'll take the back road home," Rodney said when they were all strapped in.

Toby knew the narrow asphalt road would take them longer, but he didn't answer. If he were in trouble with Anne and Newton, another hour wouldn't make any difference.

Rodney turned through a residential section that Toby hadn't even known existed and drove very slowly past the houses, most of them large and brick, with small fruit trees in the yards that showed how new they were and built-in sprinkler systems that made the new grass as green as moss. Some real-estate firm had bought all this land from a bankrupt farmer and cut down the woods between the fields and sold quarter-acre lots for thousands of dollars to people who suddenly saw the possibility or the need to live in a ritzy neighborhood.

"This is the prettiest place I've ever been," Stella said, peering out the window at the landscape of split-levels and fake Tudors.

"That's the Lawrences' house there," Rodney said, nodding toward a brick colonial where two men were working on the lawn, one riding a mower that spit grass into the air and the other weeding azaleas that still bloomed in July. "They're the same family of Lawrences that founded this town. To-bacco rich, they are. This one owns the warehouse where Daddy does business. You'd never know who he is, the way Mr. Lawrence is always smiling and joking. Acts just like everybody else."

"And you know him?" Stella asked.

"Sure. I see him all the time. Even been in that house once."

"You've been in there?" Stella was straining to look back at the house as if it were a castle about to vanish.

"Well, in the kitchen. Daddy and me went there on business with Mr. Lawrence. They've got an oven set into a brick wall. I think it's one of those that cooks anything you want in minutes. Microwave."

"I never heard of such a thing," Stella said. "He's making it up, isn't he, Toby?"

"I'm not," Rodney said before Toby could reply. "I do most all the cooking at home, and I know a lot about kitchen equipment."

"Why, Rodney, you're just—well, amazing, that's what."

Rodney had awed himself and he watched the road closely while a blush crept up his neck. Toby was silent, feeling the sudden separateness that had arisen like a wave between himself and Stella.

At home in the driveway, Rodney stopped the car and Toby got out. Dusk was falling and the lights were on at Newton's.

"I'll go tell Mr. Newton we're back," he said to Stella.

"Okay," she said, not even moving to get out. "See you tomorrow."

Toby went across the yard and around the house to the back door, away from them, where he pressed the bell hard and listened for Anne's moving in the house. A breeze was coming up, a cool, light wind that could bring a summer storm with it. He looked up. Clouds were forming in ugly, swift-moving patterns across the hazy sky.

"Well," Anne said through the screen. "You got her home all right?"

"We got a ride up with Rodney Biggers," Toby said humbly. "Stella wanted to go for a ride in his car. He's real careful, Miss Anne.

"It's all right, Toby. We weren't ready to call the sheriff yet. But next time, you arrange to come home with Newt. I'll make that clear to Stella."

"Yes, ma'am," Toby said, turning into the darkness. He didn't think there'd be a next time.

Chapter Five

Mae pulled the stopper out of the kitchen sink and stood the baby up while the soapy water gurgled around her chubby feet and down the drain. Lissy's body was tanned except for beneath her diaper, and there she seemed so vulnerable and white that Mae hurried to wrap her in a towel and take her in her arms.

There had been little time for affection in Mae's life. She'd never grown accustomed to touching people when she was a child, and so when her own children came she didn't know how to cuddle them without feeling conspicuous and foolish. But now that closeness didn't mean four in a bed or packed into the car, she was beginning to find pleasure in Lissy, her only baby now that Earl was beyond her protective grasp. Lissy was the prettiest of her children, better looking by far than Stella, who had a sharp aggressive face that told Mae she could never be satisfied.

That look of arrogance about Stella frightened Mae. Add the house—this stability James Earl seemed to relish—to Stella's determination, and Mae felt a fear growing in her, like a pain in her joints that could move up her body until it finally stopped her heart.

All her life Mae had wanted to hide, and her migrant existence had meant she could. There were so many people on the road that nobody noticed you. But now Stella wanted to be noticed, and her needing that already made her dangerous to Mae.

Like painting the house. She'd been determined and she'd done it. Even gotten that boy of Silas's to help her, and now she's off somewhere with him finding something else to do, Mae thought.

Not that she worried about Stella taking care of herself. What she didn't like was that Stella was always a bother, always giving Mae something to think about. She wouldn't be ignored, even when she wasn't there.

Stella's face came to Mae, buzzed in her brain like a nasty fly in the room. Why couldn't Stella leave everything alone? Too often lately, Mae could see James Earl in her as clear as day. Sometimes seeing Stella forced her to acknowledge that she hadn't known James Earl when he was a boy, hadn't followed the path that led him to Florida and into the diner where she was waiting tables during the waitover between orange and tomato picking. God knows, she remembered him a lot of times since— not just how he looked in that airman's uniform, as blue as sapphires he seemed. True blue. Well, he'd turned out all right, too.

When she'd hated the Air Force base, that concrete-block apartment building they had to live in, he had turned down reenlistment, although other people thought he was crazy. He'd gone on the road with her, battling the highway like it was the enemy he'd been trained to fight.

He hadn't minded the work, either. He was a farm boy, that was for sure. He knew the soil, and even when the babies grew in her, one after another as regular as a time bomb, he hadn't been angry or complained, but had just moved on from place to place—strange shack towns that got familiar just because one field looked like another after a while.

Sure, maybe she wouldn't have lost those other babies if they'd lived in a house and she'd seen a doctor regularly. But there wouldn't have been money for that, anyway, and she didn't like doctors. The one that came when she miscarried last had seemed mad at her because the blood wouldn't stop. She had no use for doctors. All spruced up in white like they expected the whole world to be clean and shiny too.

Still, she hadn't given any thought to James Earl having a home like this or a family like Newton and Anne who believed in taking what they could get. They were grabbing folks who just accumulated more and more. Like all this furniture from their attic. Why hadn't they sold it or given it away? No, they kept things. And they'd keep Stella.

Mae had seen Anne watching her, had seen her fitting that blue dress, which did improve Stella's looks even if it was a hand-me-down. Anne wanted to take Stella over, Mae thought, and she was welcome to her—except that Mae had the right of ownership to so few possessions that she couldn't let go easily.

They're taking James Earl too, she thought suddenly and squeezed the baby to her breasts. Sure as the world, they're taking him and I'll be left with nothing.

Lissy tugged at Mae's hair. "Quit that," she said so

sharply that Lissy's face puckered and she began to cry.

"It's all right, baby," Mae crooned remorsefully. "Mama's sorry. Mama's sorry." She rocked the baby gently in the straight-backed kitchen chair.

Outside, she heard voices. Stella and a strange high-pitched voice she couldn't put a face to. Who could it be? she wondered irritably.

So Stella was making friends. She had said she would. Mae remembered the first day they'd come down here to this house, her and Stella, and how Stella had said she'd never leave. She remembered herself crying, and now she felt the tears coming again.

Why can't I be like Stella? she wondered. Why can't I fit in here and not have this bad feeling like we're doing something terrible staying here? I ought to be glad for what Anne's doing. Anne had never for a minute been condescending, had never seemed sorry they'd come.

"But I've got to get outa here," Mae whispered into Lissy's clean sweet hair.

Her children had never been so clean before, had never been less than three in a bed, never eaten sweet corn or broccoli from a garden. They'd never been to an indoor movie or to church. But still, with a desperation that clung heavy in her chest, Mae Willis wanted to go. Not back to any place she'd ever been, not back to the field shacks or the one-room apartments in sultry cities that all looked the same, but away from a life that would require something of her, make her somebody if she would only let it. She smothered the soft head of her baby in her arms, wishing she could take the good things life was offering her. And the sleepy baby nestled, searching for milk that wasn't there.

Stella heard them in the night. Lying on the yellow-flowered mattress that she knew must hold some secret of its own, her body flat and straight, arms at her sides as if she were a barricade to keep Baby Earl who slept beside her from falling off, she listened to the night sounds in the next room.

Stella couldn't remember ever sleeping a wall away from her parents before. It was a strange, light feeling to be separated from them, with only Earl to share her bed and William on the cot across the room.

The house was so big to Stella. Spilled with moonlight from the open window and the door that led onto the side porch, the room seemed tremendous and gave her such a feeling of lightness and space that she wanted to stretch herself and roll on the bed, laughing aloud with delight.

From the next room, separated by the sheetrock wall and a half-closed door, sounds crept toward her. Stella lay very still, listening more closely than ever before because the sounds seemed different from those which had long been a familiar part of the night.

The wall between them made the difference. Before now, she would hear the words, feel the bed quiver and the room tumble. Then she would hear the long silence, the hush of breathless sighs, and smell the damp night smells of semen and sweat. Now the words were inaudible; they had become moans banging into a thin wall.

The bed creaked loudly. James Earl was up and passing through the room. His body was white and shining in the door light as he went naked down the porch and into the kitchen. Stella didn't move. Through the open door she could hear her mother talking. She listened, straining ears so unaccustomed to distance, to hear the words. At first she thought their noises had awakened the baby and that Mae was comforting her, but Lissy was quiet.

Stella shut her eyes and breathed lightly. The words came to her over her breath, barely audible in the darkness: "Oh, Jesus, let me keep him," her mother was saying.

Stella held her breath. She felt air moving; the screen door opened, and James Earl leaned over her. His cool hand touched her cheek, her hair. There was love in his hand. Stella struggled to be still and felt the sheet being gently laid across her quivering stomach.

"God loves you, Stella," James Earl whispered. It was a fact, the way he said it.

James Earl went softly across the room. Stella opened her eyes and watched the movement of his buttocks, the muscles of his back angling, the free swing of his arms. Because there had been little chance for privacy among them, she had seen him naked many times, and she loved his body consciously. When he hugged her as he sometimes did, lifting her off the ground against him, she loved the tension of his muscles, the hardness of his chest and stomach, the solidity of him.

The bed creaked again as James Earl eased into bed next to Mae, who lay still, her prayer still quivering on her lips. Even during their love-making, she had borne with his weight a heavy fear of losing him.

He was good to her because he was a good man. That one thing she understood. His gentleness was as inherent as the blue marble of his eyes, the shape and touch of his wiry hands. Mae shut her eyes but the tears rimmed her lashes, and she muffled a trembling sob.

James Earl, already half-asleep but stirred by her sigh, rolled into her, his head against her thin shoulder, pinning her to the ancient mattress. A pain lodged in her bones and she pressed her lips together. His breath, warm and slightly liquored, fell on her bare breasts. It was a gentle breeze, but it chilled her through the long night.

Chapter Six

In early June, just weeks before James Earl and his brood came, Anne Willis met with the high-school principal in his office and resigned from the teaching job she'd had for three years because she was expecting a baby.

The pregnancy had been planned. Conception in late winter; birth in the fall. A baby weaned by the time school started again the next year, in case she wanted to teach again that soon. She really couldn't imagine not working while she reared a family. She liked being as busy as she'd been when she was teaching and remodeling the house at the same time. She'd hardly found time then for bridge and the monthly social gatherings of their church group, and she'd enjoyed saying so.

Just being a Willis could have kept Anne busy. Her life hinged on her reputation as a wife, teacher, decorator, and social planner, and she did everything well, with such efficiency that the other young wives were helpless beside her. Yet they liked her. "She's a home-ec major, you know" was the standard explanation for why Anne Willis was perfect in every way.

Anne, for herself, knew she could do anything confidence would allow, and having Newton Willis fall in love with her had given her such a sense of accomplishment that the possibilities of her life now seemed limitless.

Not that she hadn't always felt that good things were waiting in the wings. She had recognized all the turning points readily, had felt herself becoming pretty beneath her skin and then blossoming, much like a flower she believed, until finally, in her sophomore year of college while she was serving up spaghetti in the church kitchen, Newton Willis asked her out, plucking her as if she were truly the most perfect rose in the garden.

She was wearing a white crepe blouse and a light blue pleated skirt that night, and she lifted the steaming spaghetti carefully onto the plates with two forks and then passed them down to DeeDee Johnson, who ladled the sauce on and passed them through the serving window to a table in the recreation room. Anne had intended to be out in the recreation room herself serving coffee, but then DeeDee had spilled a plate of pasta and Anne had gone in to supervise the kitchen. She was just grateful not to be serving the sauce, for being apronless she couldn't have prevented the tiny splatters that already decorated DeeDee's shirtwaist.

Anne was wearing her best clothes because she knew Newton Willis would be there, but now with the steam from the spaghetti pot rising in her face and tiny sprigs of auburn hair curling crazily about her damp head, she almost hoped she wouldn't see him. For a month, since the last church supper when she'd sat next to him at the table, she'd been half expecting him to call her. He'd implied as much when they'd finished the meal and she rose to help in the kitchen.

"Do you have to?" he'd asked, as if he didn't want the time with her to end.

"I promised," she said breathlessly. She'd hoped he'd say more, something like "Can't you get a replacement!" or "How long will you be?" But he didn't, only stood up himself and said, "Well, I'll see you later," and went off with some boys.

Anne had taken his parting words literally, so for a week she jumped when the phone rang, until her initial excitement fell slowly into a dull memory of her longing to go out with the best-looking boy in Montreet County.

Now she glanced through the serving window and saw his mother, tall and growing thin, her graying hair curled tightly around her weathered face. It was the hollow, bony face of a farm woman that smiled almost unwillingly, as if pleasure embarrassed her.

Behind her stood Newton. They stopped in front of the plates of food, and Anne saw him touch his mother's shoulder. She turned her head toward him, looking over her shoulder. She began to smile slowly, the wrinkles of her cheeks moving up to the hollows of her eyes. Newton was saying something to her and the girl serving them. The girl and Newton laughed and his mother continued to smile, her face coloring under a lingering summer tan.

Anne stood staring at them through the window, until suddenly Newton's glance caught hers, and for a second they looked at each other through the white steam from the spaghetti pot. Anne quickly turned back to her work, and when she looked again, Newton and his mother were gone.

Anne lifted the pasta resolutely, putting her mind to her task. So Newton Willis wasn't interested. So what, then? She was just nineteen years old and had almost three years left in college. She had time, and if it wasn't Newton Willis, there'd be someone else, probably somebody with a college degree if she'd just be patient about it.

Newton Willis wasn't even going to college, not that that mattered when you'd inherited a nice farm and were smart enough to make money from it. People were already talking about what kind of success Newton was headed for. He took night courses in farm management at the technical school and worked hard all day with a passion for success. At twenty, he was turning the place to a profit.

"And, thank God, Hannah is living to see it," people said, remembering the hard times since that boy James Earl went off and joined some branch of the military service, leaving old Willis and Newton to do all the work, with Newt just a boy and old Willis practically an invalid after his stroke. Old Willis had gotten more and more ornery as his mind stumbled about, until finally Newton had to act like a parent handling a stubborn, willful child who hobbled around in the fields as if he were chasing the tractor, refusing to behave himself.

Hannah had suffered and grown old and thin, sickly herself under the strain of not being able to do anything about her husband and her sons but watch. James Earl never came back, not ever, not even for his daddy's funeral; and Newton had to give up things, like playing baseball when he was the best hitter Montreet High ever had, because somebody had to work those spring afternoons. Those things had hurt Hannah, and she'd looked on helplessly, doing the little chores mothers do when they want to make up for things they can't change. She spent her social security money buying Newt nice clothes and let him take the car whenever he wanted. She never asked him for anything or nosed into his business. She cooked him good hearty dinners, when she would have eaten cheese and crackers herself. The only thing she would have asked of him was that he go to church, and he did that without being asked, probably because he knew it pleased her.

All in all, Newton Willis was practically perfect, and very attractive besides. That's what Anne Atwood was thinking when he came into the hot kitchen, his dark hair brushed carefully across his forehead and his skin smelling of English Leather.

"Hi." He was standing next to her at the stove.

"Be careful," Anne said. "DeeDee's dangerous with that sauce."

DeeDee giggled. "You better get out of here, Newton," she said.

"Not till Anne says I can drive her home," said Newton.

"I have to clean up afterward."

"I'll do it for you," DeeDee said.

"She'll do it for you," said Newton.

"Well," Anne hesitated for effect. "Well, all right then."

"Now get outa here, Newton Willis. We're busy," DeeDee said with a silly laugh.

"See you later," Newton said into Anne's ear and was gone.

"Newton Willis could have any girl in Montreet County," DeeDee said as happily as if he'd asked to take her home.

I wonder what will happen? Anne thought, lifting the spaghetti into the colander. She had always known what her life was about. She'd even reserved a place for Newton Willis, if he were interested. We'll date a few times and that'll be the end of it, she thought, knowing all the time that given the chance she'd spend the rest of her life with him.

Chapter Seven

Rodney rode with his left elbow jutting out the window and his right hand gripping the top of the wheel. Pressing his foot on the accelerator, he felt the blue Impala pick up, the hot wind from the window whip up his sleeve and around his head. The speedometer's red arrow edged toward sixty and Rodney smiled. The feel and power of the car were beginning to have an exhilarating effect on him, and he felt his fingers relax on the wheel as the car responded to his lightest touch.

The Impala sped along the country road toward the Willis farm. During the past two weeks, he'd driven the car down this road more times than he could count; now the car seemed to know the road. The bursts of heavy shade and sunlight, the silvery shimmer of the blacktop were familiar to the car itself, and Rodney leaned back, almost stretching, while his fingers hovered around the wheel.

He was happy. Gradually his summer was taking shape without his doing a thing but making himself available. He was accommodating, that was all. Stella Willis seemed to be taking care of the rest.

Like the first time he'd taken her for a ride after their jaunt to Lawrence. She'd sat on her feet, the seatbelt hanging to the floor, not in open defiance of Jean Biggers' commandment so much as just putting what she wanted first without regard for regulations. The rules were meaningless for Stella.

"Let's open the windows!" she'd shouted over the radio.

He hadn't known what to say. He'd never driven without the protection of closed windows, and now she wanted to strip it away and let the smells and sounds of summer blow in around him with the wind.

"Sure," he said finally because no other answer came to him in so few words. He switched off the air conditioner and Stella bounced on the seat, her arm out the window as if she were giving signals, her hair flying all the way to Lawrence.

Now it was Saturday again, and Rodney had the car and ten dollars he intended to put to good use. Just the day before yesterday he'd been sitting on the Willises' front porch between Stella and Toby eating the blackberries she and Toby had picked, and he had felt a pang of jealousy that told him he had to do better than just taking her into town to the soda shop. What really galled him was that she seemed to have the same kind of good time with Toby that she had with him. And Toby was always around, so that after Rodney had gotten home and he thought back on the time he'd spent with Stella, there wasn't much that didn't include Toby. Of course, he knew Toby was no threat to him—he hadn't even thought of it in those terms—it was just age and their living nearby that made Toby her friend.

Besides, long before school started in September he intended to be more than a friend to Stella. They'd be going steady by then, even though Stella was just in junior high. There wasn't anything wrong with a two-year age difference. If the truth were known, Stella acted older than Rodney felt.

Still, his concern about Toby's constant presence had caused Rodney to do some careful planning about this particular afternoon. In his shirt pocket he carried a list of places of interest, some marked through with a pencil and some circled for emphasis. The markings on his battered list were his mother's doing. Rodney hadn't done enough in his life not to still tell everything to her, so he'd thought nothing of soliciting her opinion of his plans. Jean Biggers wasn't at all surprised. She knew that sooner or later her Rodney would develop an interest in girls.

"God knows, I hope he does," she'd said time after time to his father since Rodney reached fourteen. Rodney had heard her say it and thought vaguely that it implied something odd about himself, but he had never asked his mother about it. He had waited, not knowing what he waited for until Stella showed up.

Toby, coming across the field of green oats toward Stella's house, saw the blue Impala pull in near the front porch and surround itself in dust. The dirt settled and Toby stopped to watch Rodney, wearing a new blue outfit, emerge from the car and go up the concrete blocks to the front porch. Stella was waiting there in her blue dress, and they sat down together on the porch glider Anne had given them.

Toby had been on his way to see Stella, but now he wouldn't go. She had been expecting Rodney.

The blue dress proved that. He thought about waiting in the oat field, as still as a statue, watching them until they got in the car and rode off, but what good would that do? Looking at them didn't change anything, didn't make him one of them any more than forcing himself to go up there would. Every time Rodney came, Toby felt left out no matter what he and Stella had been doing. He could feel Stella's attention edging away, politely he thought, so she wouldn't hurt his feelings outright, but nevertheless, slowly, purposefully turning toward Rodney Biggers. Toby turned away.

"We're going into town," Silas said when Toby was back in his own yard. "You comin'?"

"Yeah." Toby slumped on the porch, his back to the post.

"Somethin' ailin' you, boy?" Silas asked. He was wearing his Sunday suit and except for his white shirt made a picture in black and brown, as colorless as an old photograph.

"Just blues," Toby said, not wanting to lie to his father. Somehow he knew a lie, even a little one, would break a link between them that could never be repaired.

"A bright boy like you ain't got no use for blues," Silas said. He was grinning, putting on his act, bumbling for his son even though he wanted to respond differently. "Come on into town," he said. "Live it up some. Make yourself feel good."

"Daddy, when school starts I think I'll try out for the choir," Toby said. "I've been thinking about doing more things at school this year, and Miss Brasher at the church says I've got a clear voice."

"That's fine, son, just as long as you keep up your

grades. You've got to get some of that gift money for college. There ain't no other way."

"I know it, Daddy. But I need to get around some, too."

Across the field, dust rose and spun into the air.

"Rodney Biggers' taking Stella off somewhere," Toby said coolly.

"Yeah. He's hot for that girl, all right. James Earl better be watching out," Silas said. "And you better, too, son. Hell, I see you mooning around her. Y'all always off somewhere together when there ain't work to be doing. I like Stella. She's got a lot of James Earl in her, and that's mighty fine. But she's a Willis, Toby. You got to always remember that, and what's fitting is for people like the Willises and the Biggers to be under the same bit of moonlight."

Toby slapped his thighs and stood up to stop the conversation. "I'm coming with you," he said.

"We're getting a ride with James Earl in that vehicle of his," Silas said. "Probably have to push the damn thing."

They started down the path, Silas being careful not to dirty his suit and shoes and Toby taking long determined strides. He wouldn't care about Stella Willis. There's other fish to fry, he thought, and I got better things to do with my time. But where the hell was Rodney Biggers taking her? And how long would it be before he didn't care?

Stella sat in the dark car with Rodney, sensing that he wanted her to get out but not wanting to herself. She'd had a good time and didn't want it to end. Full of Kentucky Fried Chicken, then popcorn and cola at the movie theatre, she leaned back against the seat and smiled at the dark house before her.

"It was a lot of fun," she said softly. "It was the best time I've ever had."

"We could go again," Rodney said, sighing heavily. He was satisfied with the way the evening had gone, too. They'd seen John Wayne at the movies and that always made Rodney feel good, left him believing he could ram some heads together if he had a mind to. John Wayne was getting old, though. Now he had a wife or was a granddaddy or something like that in every picture, but Rodney remembered Saturday afternoons when men like John Wayne always got the girl after a lot of tough talk and a fight or two. It used to tickle him deep inside, so that he wanted to laugh out loud in the theatre when there was nothing really funny on the screen. He knew what was going to happen and knowing delighted him, but he held onto the laughter and trembled a little in his seat, gripping the padded armrest and straining not to break open with the grin that pushed at his face.

I could kiss Stella if I wanted to, Rodney thought, remembering John Wayne.

Stella was leaning back against the seat, resting as if she never intended to get out and go into the dark house. She looked like she wanted kissing, as if she had planned it to happen next. He had thought about it, too. Ever since he'd known Stella, he'd thought about kissing her. At odd moments, she popped into his head, like a jumping jack he'd once had that kept jumping whether he turned the handle or not. He didn't like that jumping jack with its silly grin and uncontrollable motion, and yet it fascinated him, tempted him somehow to touch it one more time. Thinking about Stella was like that, and it scared him even more than the toy had.

Stella sighed and stretched a little. Her arms were loose at her sides, and her face was turned slightly toward him, so he could see the little smile of pleasure that edged her lips. He knew better than to kiss a girl in a car. That was one of his mother's rules. "Kissing in cars leads to other things, and the lesson you learn comes too hard and too late," she had said in a tone that denied questioning.

So Rodney found himself wishing Stella would get out and go up on the porch where he could kiss her properly—well, decently, at least.

Stella moved suddenly and Rodney started. "What's the matter?" he asked, panic-stricken at being caught with his thoughts.

"Nothing," she said. "I guess I better go on in." She sighed again, waiting, and then pushed down the door handle.

"Okay." Rodney slipped out quickly and went around the car to help her out, but she was already standing beside the car in the moonlight, her hand still on the car handle as if she hadn't really decided to go in, but was waiting, biding her time. Rodney stood between the car and the porch feeling foolish. Finally, Stella came toward him. "I really did have a good time" she said when she reached him.

He took her arms at the elbows quickly, feeling the tiny bones joining in sinew and knobs. He was feeling the inside of her—the veins, the muscle, the delicious life beneath her soft flesh.

"Oh, Lord," he said, pulling her against him. He felt her breasts against his chest and even before he could find her mouth, her arms went around his neck, where prickly heat lay in rough powdered patches. His lips felt hers gently, and he thought suddenly that she was smiling and that her lips were imprinting a soft moist smile on his mouth. Then he felt her arms tighten and her smile relax, so that against his mouth her lips fell open and the wet warm tip of her tongue touched his teeth, ran softly against them, and then moved away as quickly as it had come. She moved away from him, letting go her arms and mouth in one instant that left him absolutely abandoned. "Night, Rodney," she said softly and went up the steps.

He stood there empty, drained by his first kiss of all expectation, of all John Wayne theatrics. No lights went on in the house. Stella had disappeared. It might have never happened except for the trembling in his legs and the knotted muscle of his heart. He went stumbling to the car and sat down heavily behind the wheel. Mechanically, he started the engine and, without looking where he was going, went home.

Stella knew the knock on the pane was Toby without seeing his face. She sighed and began rebuttoning her dress when what she wanted to do was ignore the tapping and fall into bed next to Baby Earl. She wanted to feel the kiss on her mouth all night, and now she would have to destroy it with words to Toby.

She opened the door and went out onto the side porch where he was sitting, his legs dangling over the side.

"What is it?" she asked, unwilling to sit down.

"I needed to see you. It's important." Toby looked

out at the woods because he couldn't lie straight to Stella's face.

"What is it?" She sat down next to him, still unwilling but curious. The kiss had already been destroyed. Her sleep, her dreams had fallen away when Toby opened his mouth and she answered him.

"Where've you been?" Toby asked.

"We went to Kentucky Fried Chicken and to the picture show, that indoor one where John Wayne's on. Rodney likes John Wayne."

"I saw him kissing you."

"You ought to be home in bed. It's late."

"I saw both of you," Toby said. "You kissed him. You were all tangled up with him."

"I was no such thing. Besides, it's none of your business, Toby. What makes you think it's your business, anyway?"

"I just saw it, that's all."

"Well, you should be home in bed. Then you wouldn't be over here in the middle of the night worrying yourself about it."

"It's not worrying me."

"Okay, then what's so important? You said there was something important."

"He don't love you," Toby said, gulping air over his words. "You're the first girl ever looked twice at Rodney Biggers."

"You go on home, Toby Brown," Stella said, standing up. "You don't know nothing about Rodney and me, because there's nothing to know. I don't know what the devil you're talking about."

"He don't care about you, that's all," Toby said stubbornly. "I'm just telling you the truth."

"And you know all about it, I reckon," Stella said. "You been places and had girl friends and kissed them all lots of times, and you know all about everything."

Toby got up and brushed off his pants methodically. "I never kissed nobody," he said slowly. "I've never been places or had girl friends. I've never done anything in my whole life that counts, but just one thing. I love you, Stella. I really do." He jumped off the porch and before she could answer, disappeared into the wooded darkness.

With a gentle pressure of her hands against the nylon of her first nightgown, Stella could make her small breasts change shape. She had been thin and awkward for so long that this sudden softness, even so small a budding as the beginning growth of breasts, gave her infinite pleasure and she stood, her shoulders arched back, her chest pushed forward against the pink sheerness of the gown, with the brown nipples pressed flat against the cloth.

I am a real person, she thought without really thinking that. Her thoughts were really on Toby, because she knew he was out there in the night, wandering probably but not really lost because he couldn't get lost in a place so familiar to him.

Stella pulled her hair back, and fine yellow wisps slipped from her hand and framed her face. The pink gown, a gift from Anne, had a lacy collar and with her free hand Stella pulled up the collar until it stood around her thin neck. She looked like somebody now. Like a girl from long ago, come back to haunt the world, to haunt Toby. But a girl like that couldn't change, could stay the same forever and ever, and Stella knew she was changing. She let her hair fall and turned down the collar.

I'm supposed to grow up, she thought, her face making a pale pout in the mirror. I'm supposed to like boys and go places with them. I'm supposed to let Rodney kiss me and kiss him back if I want to.

Even Anne, who knew all about growing up from psychology books, had explained that to her. Anne wanted Stella to understand how natural it all was. Natural, she kept saying, as if she were trying to convince Stella without being convinced herself. Stella couldn't imagine Anne being her age or starting the confounded bleeding that turned her guts inside out with cramps. She couldn't see Anne and Newton necking or going to bed together. Still, Anne was pregnant. Anne had explained that, too, had called it "being in the family way," until Stella interrupted her with a wild, delighted laugh.

"You and Newton made a baby," she laughed because she was happy for them.

She'd seen more about making and having babies than Anne Willis could have ever explained, no matter how many books she read. Stella knew the bad things, the despairing look of a woman carrying a child she didn't want and couldn't afford; the gentle apologetic face of a man who believed himself the villain without the will or the sense to change it.

She'd seen two babies born—Baby Earl who'd been stuck and kept Mae screaming for hours until finally a doctor, looking tired and disgusted, had come and turned the poor fellow right. She'd seen Lissy born, too—Lissy, who had slipped into her own hands—these two trembling, white hands that now clutched the folds of a nylon nightie. Lissy had come so quick, and Stella, alone and stunned by the birth cry of a half-grown baby, had had to do something and so had done everything. She had done things Anne Willis couldn't even imagine.

But this situation with Toby—it was something new that needed explaining. Toby had said he loved her and at that moment, with the memory of a mouth against hers, with the feel of teeth still on her tongue and the faint odor of Old Spice on her cheek, she had thought he meant he wanted to kiss her like Rodney had. But he hadn't even come near her. He'd slunk off in the dark like he was ashamed.

Well, he ought to be, Stella thought. After all, Toby and I are friends. He's the best friend I've ever had. So what he meant when he said he loved me was that he wants good things to happen to me, like Daddy does when he kisses my face and says, "God loves you." That's what Toby meant.

She flipped off the light and went down the porch into the bedroom. Baby Earl was sprawled across the bed, and she got on her knees on the mattress and moved him gently, his legs first, then his trunk, then his head. Her fingers lingered on his soft, warm body. During the day, Earl was fierce, wild, and tightly drawn at play. There was no softness in him, until sleep came and he relaxed, giving his small restless body time-out.

Stella lay down on her back next to him and looked at the ceiling. The moon was behind the woods now so the house was very dark. She lay hearing the breathing, the sighing, the calmness of sleep around her. Suddenly she was very lonely. Tears sprung into her eyes and she wished she hadn't sent

Toby away. She wished she had him near, with his hand to hold. Baby Earl moved restlessly, trying to find his original position. Stella let him move in against her and when she had wrapped him in her arms, she went to sleep.

Chapter Eight

Anne Willis watched the Impala's taillights fade into the night and turned her head back toward the tenant house, which remained dark. In her own darkness, she leaned against the windowsill and smoked, blowing the white stream against the windowpane.

Newton lay asleep across the room, his face buried in the pillow like an ostrich in the sand.

That's what he is, Anne thought, an ostrich. He doesn't see what's happening because he isn't looking. Nobody is looking but me.

There's Stella, fourteen years old and just beginning her life, already going off with boys and coming home late, with nobody up to make sure she comes in at all. And there's Toby, mooning around like anybody with eyes could see, stuck on Stella. Anne sighed and crushed out her cigarette.

She felt protective of Stella, more of her than of the other children who probably needed her more. But there was a wildness in Stella, a spirit that Anne had never had and which attracted her. How she admired the way Stella took on life, flipping her head at it as if beckoning a challenge. Stella was brimming with strength and wildness, and Anne wanted to mother that willfulness and turn it to some good purpose.

She pressed her hands against her belly. A baby grew there. Daily, nightly, in the stillness of that unborn world, a person lived. Not knowing who the baby was frustrated Anne. How could she be expected to plan for the unknown? But Stella was different. She was here and now, and the maternal feelings that Anne would have with the birth of her baby spread themselves like a crescendoing ache at the thought of Stella.

My back hurts, Anne thought. Six months along and already aching. She leaned closer to the window and caught in the moonlight the shadow of someone moving. Toby howling at the moon, roving wild in the night, not knowing he's trapped in a land he'll never own. She could see to it that Toby went to college, though. She and Newton had already talked about it and had decided if Toby couldn't get a good scholarship, she and Newton would pay his tuition and books if Silas could supply the rest. She wanted Toby to succeed because she couldn't tolerate waste. His mind gone static would be such a terrible waste that Anne would free him if she could.

But I'll have to talk to Mae about him, she thought. She's so stupid, she'll never see, not about Toby or Rodney Biggers, either. Oh, I wish I could just sleep and not think about anything.

A light came on in the tenant house. It shone from the small, high bathroom window, and looking down into it, Anne could see a blur of pink. Stella in her nightgown. Anne frowned. It won't keep her warm, she thought. Stella will need more than a summer gown. The time will come when she'll need so much more.

Anne went back to bed and slipped under the sheet next to Newton. He didn't stir, and she moved closer to him, her face near his cheek, her hand on his hip.

"The north wind doth blow and we shall have snow and what will poor robin do then, poor thing?" she whispered into his ear.

"Huh?" Newton muttered in his sleep. He turned, pulling away from her, and Anne lay still, the rhyme still on her lips and spinning through her head. "What will the robin do then," she sang herself to sleep.

The bedroom next to Anne and Newt's had been designated the nursery, and on the weekdays when there was no tobacco ready for barning, Stella went up to the big house to help Anne get ready for the baby. James Earl offered to return the crib he and Newton had slept in and that now was Lissy's, but Anne wouldn't hear of it. She wanted everything new and shiny, so she took Stella into Lawrence and they picked out furniture and material and paint, all with Stella's approval. Anne even let her pick out an outfit, white trimmed in yellow so either a boy or girl could wear it home from the hospital, and toys, a fluffy stuffed lamb wearing a straw hat and a mobile of bright butterflies to hang over the crib. Stella had never thought of planning for a baby, and she entered the preparations with enthusiasm, forever thinking of new things they should get from the advertisements she saw in the baby magazine Anne already subscribed to.

"She's spending too much time up there," Mae said to James Earl. "She's bothering 'em."

"No, she ain't. Newton told me just yesterday how much Anne's enjoying Stella's helping her. When you get right down to it, Stella knows more about babies than a lota folks."

"Not about what Anne's doing, she don't. Stella knows about makin' 'em and the pain of gettin' 'em into the world, but she don't know a thing about furniture and all that."

"Then she's learning something," James Earl said. "It ain't hurting nothing, Mae." He stirred his mashed potatoes with his fork.

Mae sat down across the table with Lissy on her knees and spooned potatoes into the baby's mouth.

"Lissy can feed herself," James Earl said. "You oughta let her."

"Anne says Stella's too young to go off with that Biggers boy," Mae said, holding a glass of tea up to Lissy's mouth. The baby gulped and turned her mouth from the glass.

"What'd you say to her?" James Earl stopped eating and looked at his wife.

"I said I didn't know." Mae sniffed and put the baby on the floor. "I can't talk to Anne. You know that."

"Stella's smart. She knows better than to get into trouble," James Earl said.

"Well, Anne says Toby likes her too much, too. She says we ought to know about it."

"Hell, Mae, Toby's as good as they come. Anne's just worrying about things ain't hers to worry about. She's been to college and all and thinks she's up a notch or two. Stella's nothing to worry about."

"She ain't perfect, James Earl. She's growing up, got the pip and all. She could get a baby." Mae blew her nose.

"Stella's all right," James Earl said. He got up and went to the back door. "Stella's all right, you hear?"

"I hear," Mae said when the screen had shut and James Earl's brogans had hit the dirt beside the porch.

Courage accompanied by pride came to Rodney Biggers just as his mother had predicted. She had been known to say that habitual sin could begin looking virtuous. That was sort of what happened to Rodney. Not only that, now he wanted to get more expert at sin.

At first, just the sight of Stella Willis had him shivering, and then touching her arm and her hand made his heart race, and then came kissing—quick tongue kisses that got longer and longer, until he was feeling not just tongue and lips and teeth, but the softness of her breasts against his chest and their coming fullness as his hands moved beneath her arms when she stretched to reach around his damp neck. For a while, kissing was all Rodney thought about; then kissing wasn't enough.

"Rodney's getting itchy," Jean Biggers said to her husband, who wasn't listening. "He's going off with that Willis girl three or four nights a week, and I can just tell he's getting itchy. You're not listening. I'm here trying to have a serious conversation with you about your son, who, thank God, is not queer, and you aren't even doing me the courtesy of listening."

"What's to say?" Mr. Biggers said over his *Farm Journal*. "Every normal boy God made gets itchy. He's just got to adjust."

"I tell you, Frank, it's getting serious. Rodney is a serious boy and he takes things seriously. He thinks he's in love with this little Willis girl, and we both know what that can lead to."

"Rodney's had a good upbringing. I trust him to behave himself."

"You ought to have a talk with him," Jean said. "You ought to make sure he understands everything."

"Jean," Mr. Biggers said, "there's nothing I could possibly tell Rodney that you haven't told him already."

Stella handed tobacco under the barn shelter, standing next to her mother and handing her bunches to Synora, who tied them quickly on the stick with twine that ran from a ball hanging on a post. For the past two weeks, since the night Toby had seen her kissing Rodney and had told her he loved her, Toby had avoided her. When he brought the full truck into the shelter, he didn't look at her, but talked gaily to the black girls on the other side of the wagon, making jokes that sent them roaring with laughter. Stella knew she was being left out and that sooner or later she and Toby would have to come to terms with each other, but at the moment she was living in the pleasure of helping Anne plan for the baby and being Rodney Biggers' girl. So she ignored Toby's subtle glances in her direction and pretended not to hear the talk between him and the other girls.

All day she stood there handing tobacco, barefooted in her faded shorts, an old T-shirt of Newton's, and her first bra.

Anne had taken her into the only ladies' store in town a few days ago, back into a little room with a brass and velvet chair in it and a tremendous mirror on the wall and an aqua damask curtain in place of a door. Then she'd said, "Take off your dress and try this on."

She'd held out a brassiere, dangling it by the lacy white straps, and Stella had stood motionless, stunned by the sheer beauty of it, and then had reached out her hand and touched it, felt the soft white padding in the small cups, touched the tiny blue flower in the middle with a shaky hand.

"Am I big enough?" she'd whispered, still touching it and not beginning to undress.

"I think so. We'll try it and see," Anne had said gaily, unable to hide her own delight at seeing Stella's excitement.

Stella had undressed quickly then and slipped the bra on, turning toward the mirror while Anne hooked the back, looking at herself in yellowed cotton panties and the gleaming white cups that seemed to make her breasts grow inside them, filling them impossibly. "It fits," she'd said breathlessly. "I fill it up!" She laughed and locked her hands in front of her so that the flesh above the lacy rim seemed even larger. Then she'd grabbed Anne and hugged her for the first time, dancing and trying to swing her around in the tiny room.

"You can wear it home then," Anne had said, laughing with her. "And I'll get you nylon panties and a new slip, maybe even another gown if you see one you like."

Stella had put on her clothes and felt completely, newly dressed, not yet hampered by the contraption around her chest, but made freer than ever by this undeniable fact of her growing up.

So now she wore the bra under Newton's T-shirt and knew that everybody, Toby included, could see it. The black girls didn't wear bras although they were bigger than Stella, having already the shape of women, with rounded breasts and hips.

Toby noticed the bra, the white outline of it clear as day through the shirt, and he turned away, not wanting to see that she was changing. Every day she grew farther away from him. Under the shelter, he watched her slyly and then sometimes bluntly just to see if she'd look him straight in the eye, challenging her to face what he'd told her about himself. Loving Stella was the hardest thing he'd ever done, and he longed to have her know that, not because it was a weakness in him, but because he believed it showed his strength. He could love her and leave her alone, which was something Rodney Biggers obviously couldn't do. Rodney was there almost every night, kissing her, mauling her, taking her God knows where in that car of his. Rodney was using her, learning from her and on her, whether Stella would admit it or not.

"That's what a whore's for," Silas had told him not long ago. "To learn from. You don't go messing around no nice girl till you know what's going on with your own self."

"I don't want to mess around at all," Toby had said, angry that his daddy would bring the subject up when he was already distraught with thoughts of Stella.

"Time'll come when you will, son, and this is just a little advice to think on. I ain't promising I'll be around when the time comes."

"You sure as hell won't," Toby'd said under his breath as he walked home in front of Silas. He had never cursed at his daddy before, not even in his head, and he suddenly wanted to turn back and say,

"I'm all right. Everything's all right," because he knew his daddy saw what he wanted to hide. But he couldn't, and he didn't; just went home fast, into his room where he shut the door and lay on his bed, his hands clenched behind his head, holding themselves together so tightly that his bones ached, keeping them away from where he longed to touch.

Chapter Nine

The dawn was wet. Dew lay heavy on the grass when the eastern sky turned ripe, bursting with sunlight beyond the trees, and James Earl, stepping high as if to keep his feet dry, crossed the yard to Newton's back door.

He went quietly up the steps, wiped his wet brogans on the mat that read "Willis Welcome," and slipped into the kitchen where the lights were still on and Newt leaned over the sink, half a waffle dripping with syrup in his hand.

"Breakfast," he said, shoving the rest of the waffle in his mouth and draining his coffee cup. "You eat yet?"

"Coffee's all I wanted," James Earl said, sitting down at the table. He hunched his shoulders as if he were shivering, although the morning was already warm and he was wearing a ragged khaki jacket over his work clothes.

"Want some more?" Newt offered. "Anne's still in bed. She's got a backache about half the time, especially at night, so she doesn't sleep much anymore." He poured James Earl a mug of coffee and set it in front of him.

"The pickup's under the packhouse shelter, and

Silas is up there clearing off the place to put the load," James Earl said, embracing the mug with his fingers. "You ever feel cold right down through your bones?"

"Yeah," Newton said. "When I've been tramping in those woods out there for three hours in twenty-degree weather and ain't seen a squirrel yet."

James Earl laughed, although his brother wasn't really affecting his seriousness. "I've been that kind of cold, too," he said solemnly. "One time, Daddy and me went deer hunting up near Smithfield, Virginia. He was in one blind and I was in another. I just about froze my ass off and didn't see a deer all day. Finally, I went over to see if Daddy wasn't ready to call it quits, and there he was, nursing a bottle of whiskey and as warm as toast. Shit, he couldn't of hit a buck if one had stopped ten feet in front of him, but I was damn lucky he didn't get a shot off at me."

Newt laughed but then, seeing that the recollection of their father seemed to trouble James Earl, became quiet. Their father seemed to Newton to have always been an old man—not tottering as he had been in those last years after a stroke broke his mind and scattered it aimlessly in the past, but humorless, arbitrary, unaffectionate toward his sons, as if he believed love was a weakness they should all conquer.

Newton didn't like this memory of his father and felt himself somehow responsible for it, so he turned his attention back to James Earl.

"Something bothering you?" he asked.

"I need to talk to you," his brother said slowly.

"The season's almost over," Newt said. He moved back to the sink and stood looking at the sun, which was mellowing in the sky, spreading itself across the horizon like apricot nectar. "Two more weeks, maybe less, and we'll have the tobacco in. Then the women'll have to get to the grading in a damn hurry."

"Mae don't know a thing about grading tobacco," James Earl said.

"She can learn," Newt said. "And Stella can take off sticks for 'em."

"Well, I was gonna ask you about our staying on a few weeks," James Earl said. "I figured with the tobacco about in, you wouldn't be needing us much longer."

"I need you as long as you need me," Newt said, still looking at the sky, imagining himself the parent not just of the baby Anne was carrying but of his brother as well. It was a responsibility he didn't want and wasn't prepared for, yet he knew acutely that it was his. He pressed his hands against the porcelain sink rim as if its coldness could draw him away from the memory of his father. He was afraid he couldn't be different from the old man for, at that moment, he also felt the possibility of love being a weakness.

"Come winter there ain't enough to do. I know that," James Earl was saying. "You'll be supporting us and I don't want that to happen."

"There's potatoes to dig, Jimmy," Newt said. "Then there's the combining. I combine oats for just about everybody in the county. Then there's the live-stock to take care of and burning off the fields. There's enough to keep you and me and Silas damn busy till Christmas. Then, before you know it, it's seedtime again."

"I can go now, Newt," James Earl said. "I mean, after the tobacco's ready for market, before school starts and Stella gets all ripe to go, we can be gone. You say that's the best thing and I'll go."

"Stella wants to go to school in town," Newt said impatiently. "She's got that Biggers boy wrapped around her little finger, and you're here thinking about taking her off in that station wagon that probably wouldn't get ten miles down the road anyhow." Newton turned from the sink and looked at his brother. "Anne's having a baby in September. The tobacco looks damn good. Life seems to be starting all around us, Jimmy. What makes you want to back off from it?"

"I'd like to stay, Newt. God knows, it's time for me to stay somewhere. I just need for you to say it's all right. Come spring, I can plant that acreage Mama left me, if that's all right by you. Maybe make something on my own."

"Hell, yes, it's all right." Newton sat down and pulled on his brogans. He could feel the growing complexity of his life like the tangled laces Baby Earl played with. His fingers sought the knot, and it unraveled miraculously between his fingers.

"James Earl," he said as the leather slipped easily around the metal hooks, "all those years you were gone, when Mama was dying and even before that, when things were bad with Daddy and I couldn't do all the things kids think they've got to do to be somebody, I hated you for going off. Even knowing your going gave me a chance to make something of myself didn't stop me from feeling what I did. I didn't understand then how responsibility and making something of yourself go so close together. But things worked out. I got Anne, something I hadn't even dreamed about. I got lucky with the weather, and the crops came in good without my worrying myself to death. Gave me time to learn about the land and make enough to get some new equipment, like that combine machine that's been making money ever since.

"And then you come home. God damn it, James Earl, you were dragging your tail when you came in here, and I put you in that tenant house and put you to work for wages. I thought to myself, I ain't my brother's keeper. You went out and got married and got them children, and you're responsible for 'em. But then I started seeing something. All the time, I've loved you. And now I love them all, even Mae who can't look me in the face to this day, because they're yours and you're mine and together we're all that's left of the Willises."

"Silas is in the packhouse," James Earl said. His voice was quavering beyond his control. He stood up and went to the back door. "Thanks, Newt," he said, unable to look at his brother.

"It's gonna be a scorcher," Newton said, following him outside. He stopped next to James Earl on the steps and looked up at the sky. "But we might get rain by afternoon." He touched his brother's shoulder.

The dew was drying. Across the grass they went, Newton's hand resting lightly on his brother's shoulder. Under his brother's hand, James Earl felt the chill leaving him.

At one-thirty, only a little while after they'd gone back into the fields from dinner, the sky split open. Lightning, a blazing butcher knife among the wind-blown black clouds, cut jagged slices in the stirred-up sky, and rain poured from the slits as the men raced for the shelters. The women, already there at their work, stopped their bunching and tying and sat down, squatting against the barn's worn side where they talked slowly among themselves to squelch their fear of the storm.

Mae was under the shelter too, but she stood with the side of her head against the wall and stared at her bare, black feet. She was the only white woman under the shelter except for Stella, who sat in the packed dirt playing tic-tac-toe with a colored girl. They drew the game quickly, ignoring the wind that swept its chilling rain under the shelter and the thunder that shook the building sporadically. Stella wiped the ground with her hand, and they started again, the black girl marking a line on the ground next to her foot where they kept the score.

Toby was under the shelter, too, but he stood away from the girls, with his back against one of the posts, and watched them play. Down the lane under the next barn shelter, Mae could see James Earl and Silas smoking against the barn wall. She made a quick count of her children: Stella, William in an empty tobacco truck next to his daddy, Baby Earl easing up behind Stella like a bandit taking his victim by surprise, Lissy down the road in the house, hopefully sleeping through the storm.

She could account for them all. Within her vision they rested as still as photographs on the black background of the sky, and yet she couldn't accept them there, couldn't stand the black feet she stared down at or the gummy feel of tobacco juice on her hands that made her fingers stick to her skirt. The rain had brought with it a torrent of her own feelings, and she felt how much she despised the house down the

road where her baby slept and where she had a bathroom, electric lights, and oil heat for when winter
came.

Winter, she thought resentfully, as the rain whip-
ped under the shelter on the wind. I can't stay here
through the winter. I just can't.

Another gust of wind brought a sudden spray of
water against her back.

"You're getting wet, Miss Mae," Toby was saying
to her. "You're getting wet."

"I'm going in the barn," she said sharply, knowing
she had become so stationary that even these people
could interfere with her thoughts.

To escape them, she stepped over the boards into
the dark and then crossed the oil lines that divided
the dirt floor into sections. The barn held the aroma
of cured tobacco, as sweet as fruit.

"Smells just like money," Newton liked to say.

And how Mae wanted to answer him. Oh, how she
longed to look him square in the face and spit out
words that fermented like bitter vinegar in her
brain.

"I despise your goddamn tobacco," she wanted to
say. "And your house and your wife and your voice
that takes my children away because it bribes them,
yes, bribes them with clothes and toys and fancy
ideas when none of this is really theirs. We don't
want what you can give us, Newton Willis."

But she would never say that because she knew it
wasn't really true. The kids and James Earl did have
wants. Already the word was spreading through the
vocabularies of children who had never known they
needed anything beyond what was already there—a
blanket, some milk, a body next to theirs in the dark.

The interior of the barn was as black as night, but

the storm thundering above her seemed thwarted by
the asbestos siding that covered the outside of the
building. It was as dark and cool as the inside of the
car at night when they were heading for the next
picking station. She could sleep best with the tireless
whirring of the engine, the rippling highway that
rocked her as if she were a baby herself, carrying
her wherever it wanted her to go.

Toby followed Mae to the door, and a sudden
flash of lightning showed him how the chain attached to the ceiling vent wasn't hooked to the wall
as it usually was, but had been slung over the rafter
directly above Mae's head. The sight of the chain—
metal in the electric air—terrified him.

His mouth was opening to say, "Come from
under there, Miss Mae." But while the words were
still in his mouth, spinning on his sticky tongue like
dry peas, the barn was aglow with lightning. The
chain burned brightly, shooting white flame to Mae
who was white and glaring, a burning outline of herself.

Toby was falling, feeling the scorch on his own
body, smelling the sear of skin and hair, tumbling
onto the ground that shook with thunder. When he
hit the floor, he was already scrambling up, shaking
his head violently. His vision blurred as he tried to
focus on Mae, who seemed suspended between the
chain and the ground, silent, stock-still, as if para-
lyzed in her contact with fire and earth.

Toby lunged at her with the only tobacco stick he
could find, and it tore into his hand as he swung
frantically. Mae toppled over in a heap on the black
barn floor, the current suddenly as still as death.

Stella was there. All his life Toby would remember that. She was there screaming and the women

were screeching and the thunder was clapping. Everybody was running. Toby held Stella, who had appeared in the frame of white door light as Mae fell. His arms pressed her against his chest as he poured all his energy into his trembling limbs to keep her safe, because suddenly she was weaker than he.

"She's dead," Silas said over the body.

James Earl, dripping rain from his skin and clothes, knelt there while the black women held onto his sons and Toby held his daughter. He caressed the hot body of his wife tearlessly until Newton came and lifted him under his arms like a child and set him on his feet. Then Silas led him out through the drizzling rain to the house where Lissy still slept.

But Stella stayed and Toby held her limp body, which seemed boneless, melting into his own, until her weight was more than he could bear and he sank to the ground, still holding her, and she sank with him. They sat huddled together near the canvas-covered body of her mother until Newton returned with a quilt to wrap her in, with Anne running after him, calling to the women to carry the children up to the big house.

Then an ambulance came, and still Stella stayed in Toby's arms and watched, as though she were gathering every detail concerning a death. When Anne tried to loosen her from Toby's grasp, her grim refusal cut across her face like a slap, contorting her cheeks and mouth as she whispered hoarsely into Toby's chest, "No . . . no."

So after everyone had gone, she sat in Toby's arms, and he kissed her dingy white neck gently with dry, burning lips and cradled her head against his chest with an unsteady hand, smearing her with his own blood. The searing smell about his body held him as closely as he held Stella. His arms ached and the cuts in his hand drew at his flesh, pinching him unmercifully. His eyes watered and he could feel mucus collecting in his throat and nose. His body seemed to stiffen; but then the reality of Stella touched him like the feel of her breasts through her shirt, and he relaxed and let himself go in a dream of holding her forever.

When she finally stirred, it was as if from sleep, and she pulled herself away from Toby impatiently, as if he had been thwarting her real intention. Silently, she searched the darkness above her head until she made out the chain that had been burned away from the ceiling vent and hung loosely over the rafter.

"Lift me up," she said coldly.

Toby put his aching arms around her knees and hoisted her into the air until her hands grasped the chain and she sent it clanging and thumping to the ground. Then he let her down so that their heads were together and her breath heaved in his face.

"Do you think people want to die?" she whispered.

"Don't go," Toby said. "Stay here with me."

"Do you think she wanted it to happen? She didn't like it here, you know." Stella put her cheek against Toby's.

"I'll take care of you," he said, putting his arms around her again.

"I'm going to the house to see about Daddy. He needs me now." She moved away, and Toby let her go. "Don't you come with me," she said.

Toby stood in the barn door and watched her go, her T-shirt bright, her whole form white in the night. Then he went back into the barn and picked up the chain. He could feel the charred surface, the metal turned to grit beneath his cold fingers. He felt how completely the metal in his hand had changed Stella's life—more than she knew yet, even more than he knew.

All his senses were still keyed to her physical presence, the feel of her skin and hair, the fluttering of her body in his arms. She had needed someone, and he had been her comfort, at least for awhile. But he needed comfort, too. His body hurt. His mind still shook in waves of shock at the sight of Mae's electrified form. He had seen someone die. He had done all he could to save her, and it hadn't been enough.

He knew the charred chain was coating his hands. The grit stuck in his scratched palm, and he rubbed his hand on his shirt slowly as if to brand himself with failure.

Outside the sky moved slowly, still exhausted from the storm. Across the field, a light shone from his own house. Down the road, lights glowed from Stella's.

It would rain again. During the night he would shake in the darkness, needing a warmth that wouldn't come. Then there would be a funeral and a burial and a fearful sense of loss to contend with. He couldn't fathom the effect this ceremony of death would have on Stella or himself. But flowing with the current that killed Mae Willis, he sensed there must be reviving strength too.

He stepped outside the barn, dropped the chain into an empty nail keg under the shelter, and went slowly home, a shadow among so many.

Chapter Ten

Young Enright the undertaker waited by his front door to lead the Willis family down the hall to the last visiting room of his funeral home. His shiny black shoes shifted soundlessly on his new grass-green carpet as his impatience grew.

Enright didn't really like the business he'd inherited from his father. He had already endured a frustrating childhood of infuriating Enright jokes, although he had long ago admitted to himself that it was a peculiarly comic name for an undertaker to have. He had, of course, considered other occupations and had really wanted to teach in high school and maybe coach basketball, but in the end the money to be had in the family business had swayed him. He could make a good living burying people, and he'd gotten used to it, just like he'd gotten used to Enright jokes.

"Enright sure gets them in right" was the classic, corny example of small-town humor that he had to bear. But when people were serious, when they were burying their own, they didn't make jokes. No, they grasped the dry, manicured fingers Enright pushed at them gratefully and made monthly payments of whatever amount he charged.

Still, for Enright the hardest part of his job was making the loved ones of the deceased feel at ease. He knew nobody was comfortable with death. Its touch was too cold and reminded people too keenly of their own mortality. People cried out their loss, their anger, the inconvenience death caused them, and Enright had to make them comfortable no matter what rage or grief they felt.

The Willises received special treatment—the last room so no one could gawk at them; a discount price on the coffin both because Enright knew James Earl didn't have any money and because he'd already been paid more than he deserved on other Willis funerals. He'd phoned Jean Biggers, who came and tried to do something with the woman's hair when there was nothing much that could be done. She'd finally done old-fashioned finger waves that at least made the brittle, singed hair lie down.

"She just mighta been pretty once," Jean had said to Enright when she'd finished and was packing up her supplies. She spoke softly but emphatically to her ally. It was as if only she and Enright really knew Mae Willis, although neither of them had ever seen her walk a step or say a word.

"Yes," Enright whispered, ushering Jean down the hall because he knew nobody wanted to be alone in his funeral home. "We did what we could. Anne supplied the dress. One of her own." Enright smiled remembering Anne in the office sighing over the two dresses she'd brought.

"Help me decide, Fred," she'd said, holding each dress in front of her bulging stomach. One was a pink party frock; the other, a blue summer dress with tiny tucks of lace running up to its high, ruffled collar.

"That one," he had said, pointing at the blue. Mae Willis had bad shoulders and a hollow chest that needed covering. "The blue one will be fine."

Anne had sat on the vinyl sofa and folded each of the dresses carefully. Suddenly, she looked up and gave him an embarrassed smile. "Why am I doing this?" she asked and shook out the blue dress frantically.

He went over and took it from her shaking hands. "You're upset, Anne." He had a slight smile on his lips that he intended to be sympathetic. He practiced making it sympathetic, but without benefit of a mirror, he always felt it became sinister on his angular face.

Anne smiled back, but the corners of her mouth trembled. "It's the children, Fred," she said. "I didn't ever really get to know Mae, and now there are the children to think about."

"And one of your own." Fred sat down in his swivel chair and leaned back. Outside on the side proch of his funeral home, the children sat on the steps, backs and heads without faces looking into the sun.

Anne patted her stomach. "Yes, one of my own. And now this." She went to the window. "What do they know about anything, Fred? What can I say to them?"

From the quivering of her shoulders, Fred knew she was beginning to cry. "We can make her look nice, Anne, if that's any consolation. We can have a nice service for them to look back on." I'm not good at this, he was thinking while he spoke. I'll never be good at this.

Anne had seemed to sense his discomfort, and she'd turned to him. "I know you'll do a lovely job, Fred. You always do. We all appreciate that." She smiled and shuddered back her tears. "I'll be going now. I have to get the children something to wear. None of them has a thing to wear."

Now Enright watched them from the shadow of his entrance as they came up the walk—Newton and James Earl first, with Newt carrying Baby Earl and James Earl holding William's small hand firmly. Enright could see that James Earl was holding on for dear life and that the boy, his arm stretched and bent awkwardly in his father's grasp, didn't know what was happening.

At that moment, James Earl was the weaker of the two, because he did understand and was feeling his loss, the helplessness of being a man with no place to turn because his comfort was finally, undeniably gone. He was suffering and his hot, clutching hand squeezed his helplessness into his son. Newton was like a giant beside them, and he carried the smaller boy lightly and strode slightly ahead.

They came up the steps, and Enright moved silently in front of the glass door and pushed it open. The men nodded to him as they passed, and then Enright could see Anne and the two girls coming slowly. The baby waddled between them, her stumbling steps holding them back, and Anne and Stella waited patiently, letting the baby find her way.

One of them ought to be carrying that baby, he thought impatiently. She ought not to even be here at all. But that was none of his business, and he gave Anne and then Stella his sympathetic smile and rested his hand for a moment on the baby's white head.

"Come on in," he said softly to them all. They stood waiting as if they could wait forever because they didn't want to live through the hours before them. He had to lead them, to force them gently in to face the dead woman whose body they had all known in one way or another.

The body was all he could speak for, and Enright stopped inside the little room to let them pass and move in silently to the casket to look. He had learned to discern how the corpse looked to the mourners from their sighs, stifled moans, tiny throaty sobs. Now there was silence.

"Mama," William said loudly.

"Shush," James Earl said, still clutching the boy's hand.

"Mama don't have hair like that," William said. His voice seemed to come through a microphone, transmitting Enright's failure.

"She looks pretty though," Stella said.

James Earl turned away. His head was down and his body shook.

Enright stood still, watching the two brothers closing in on each other. Newton, with his broad muscular arms reaching around his brother, was the stronger, but then he hadn't lost anything this time.

"Don't let the children see you like this, Jimmy," Newton said, while William looked blankly at both of them.

James Earl straightened up suddenly and looked around for Enright.

"She looks real nice, Fred," he said, his voice warbling in his throat.

"Yes," Enright said. "A lot of people have come, James Earl. You've got a lot of friends here." He nodded toward the register next to the door.

"That's real nice," Newton said. "You want to stay here awhile longer, Jimmy? Anne and I can take the kids on out."

"No," James Earl answered and then turned back toward the casket as if his own negative response had told him what this really meant. "Stella," he said while he stared at Mae, "you ready to go home now?"

Stella had been standing close to the casket all the while, looking at her mother's face. As still as the corpse, she made herself remember what Anne had told her while she studied the finality of death.

"Mama's soul's with Jesus," she said to Baby Earl and Lissy who stood next to her, neither of them tall enough to see into the casket. "That's just Mama's shell, like a snail's shell, Earl," she said, quoting Anne. "And Mama doesn't live in there anymore."

"Where's Mama?" Baby Earl asked on his tiptoes. He was trying to peep over the edge of the casket.

"With Jesus," Stella said. "With Baby Jesus. She's his mama now too."

Earl turned away satisfied.

"Well, let's go," Stella said. "Anne, I'll carry Lissy. She's getting tired." She bent over and picked up the baby. Her legs wobbled for an instant as she balanced their bodies together.

"Let me take her," Anne said, holding out her hands.

"No." Stella passed them all as she went into the hall and down the cushioned corridor. Carrying the baby that was now hers, she led the way.

The first thing Stella noticed, the very first thing that showed itself in the summer glare that made everything around her look white and hot and wilting, was the hole itself. A frame had been set into it to support the casket, but the metal rods and rope didn't hide the emptiness of the hole or the clean, smooth, black dirt sides of it. She had expected something less methodical, a gently sloping hollow in the ground like turned earth to plant something in.

There is a difference in planting and burying, she thought, watching the casket being slid across the metal and ropes so that it was suspended above the deep hole, hovering there like it was unwilling to be let down, holding itself up by its own force and by a voice inside that cried, "No, don't."

Men were putting flowers around the box, covering the space left to look at, covering up what was happening as if they could smooth over this day. Stella shuddered, her insides as cold and clammy as the inside of the hole must be. Across the sprays of carnations and gladioli, she saw Toby dark against the white sun, and the sight of him, his head down, not looking at her but nevertheless there, made her feel better. She sniffed the scent of the flowers, seeking a human smell. Her fingers relaxed around Lissy's so that she held the baby's hand loosely and could feel the sweaty fingers that played against her palm, struggling listlessly to be free. She looked again for Toby.

There was a crowd: people she'd never seen before, friends of Newton's, people like Miss Maggie Grover, who had known her daddy when he was a boy. Rodney, who had said "Yes, ma'am" and "Thank you" to her mama because he was going off to kiss Stella, was there with his parents, his mother lacquered and shining in her summer clothes just as Stella had imagined she would look, and the father slouching, not able to stand up against the heat in his winter suit.

They all sweltered while the preacher read. Stella

pressed Lissy's hand just to make sure she herself could feel.

Standing down the row from her was her daddy, still gripping William's hand as if he were holding the boy back from the coffin, although William was pulling backward, struggling silently to run away. While the preacher prayed, Stella saw Newton step behind William and put his hands firmly on the boy's shoulders to hold him down.

Nobody cried. Across the cemetery, which was a single sloping hill of browning grass, came the smell of the town dump and the sound of rushing water from the treatment plant. The water gurgled up, a cleansing fountain beside a dying garden, and then spilled itself, spreading out clean on the surface of the reservoir. She licked her lips. She was thirsty. Her mouth tasted salty and stung her lips.

It was over. The people moved away and then came closer. They were grasping hands and saying words that made no sense to her. Maggie Grover was hovering over her, whispering something Stella didn't catch. Then Rodney Biggers was at her side, his hand firmly on her arm as if he intended to wrench her away from Lissy. "I won't go," Stella said straight to his face.

"What?" Rodney shifted his feet and released her arm. He didn't seem to know what he wanted.

"I'll come out to see you," he stammered. "When can I come?"

What was he talking about? Stella bent down and picked up Lissy, who clung to Stella's neck and her legs gripped Stella's waist.

"What do you want?" Stella asked Rodney. He was a blur in front of her, and she wished he'd move away to give her room and light.

"I just want to come and see you," Rodney said again.

"Well, do it then," she said and turned away. She held Lissy tightly, and the sweat on their dresses oozed between their separate skins.

"I'm going now," she said to the crowd in general. She started toward the black Lincoln where Enright stood holding the door open for her.

"We can come back later," he said as she got in.

"What for?" she asked him.

"I saw you there," she said to Toby that night when he came and sat on the side porch, his back to the kitchen light and his bare feet dangling above the grass. He had come without knocking or asking, just in case she needed him.

And she did. Looking through the kitchen screen at him, Stella knew she had always needed somebody like Toby, as solid, as stationary and predictable as wood and stone.

"You knew I'd be there." Toby looked into the woods.

Stella sat down next to him and put her hand on his arm. "There were all those people I didn't know, and there was you."

"And Rodney Biggers," Toby said, and wanted to snatch the words back.

"He's nice, Toby," Stella said, still touching his arm. "I know you don't like him much, but he's nice to me."

Why did she want him to understand? Why did she want him to be patient and listen? Neither of them knew. It just seemed as if that must be the way it was if they were to go on from here, if they were ever to be close again the way they were the day they painted the house and went to town.

But we didn't come home together, Toby remembered. Rodney Biggers brought them and stayed. He'll probably stay, him or somebody like him, for the rest of our lives.

As dry and aching as it made his mouth, as vile as he felt the rage beneath his crawling skin, he knew he had to face the fact that he didn't belong in Stella's world, just as he'd had to come to terms with who and what he was so many times before. At those moments, when he was forced to remember that his family had nothing behind it but a past of working somebody else's land, he wished his father had gone North years ago when there were good factory jobs for the asking. He wished they'd abandoned the South forever. What had it ever done for them?

But his daddy didn't feel that. Silas didn't think he could handle the worry of city living or working on his own, so Toby had learned to say "Yes, sir" to everything, agreeing with the bossman even when it was Mr. Newt, like he didn't have a mind at all but was a mechanical switch people pressed that beeped out recorded answers: "Yes, Miss Anne. Whatever you say."

He did that, spit out those words for his parents' sake, but he'd never given himself up to it, never doubted that he could change his life when he was old enough and smart enough. He believed with angry determination that economic and educational poverty (that's what his civics teacher called it without looking at him) were all that stood in his way. And now that the black folks were getting along better, why shouldn't he? He had to take the same risks of rejection, peel off the same layers of skin to make himself visible, active, dauntless in his quest. He would be seen and heard someday.

Stella moved closer to him. Her hand slid, unconsciously it seemed, up his arm and across his shoulder, skimming the cloth of his shirt, feeling beneath it the muscles that shivered involuntarily under her fingers.

"Oh, Toby," she sighed, her hand now on his shoulder, her arm lying heavily on his back. "I'm glad you were there to see it all. It wasn't like I thought it would be. Nothing was—not the way Mama looked or the things that preacher said or that hole they put her in. Especially that hole. It looked too big and deep, like you couldn't climb out of it if you fell in. You'd just be down there forever and ever." She leaned closer, resting her head against his shoulder so that she was embracing him. He couldn't move. Now Stella was in control, and he was lifeless, suspended in a motionless dream.

"I think Mama stood there waiting to get struck down," she said without bitterness. She sighed again and leaned heavily against him. It was as if she remembered the comfort he'd once given her and was returning to it. "I think she let it happen because she didn't like it here. And now look at what's happened. She's in that hole out there. She's in this ground forever." Stella spoke carefully as if the words themselves were her enemies and she had to base her strategy against them on their sound.

"Oh, Toby," she whispered into his neck, for the finality of her words seemed to defeat her. Her breath slipped inside his shirt collar, enveloping him like a scented cloud. "Oh, Toby."

He was kissing her. At first his mouth felt tight and hot, but then her lips seemed like water on his, her face like a pool he could dip into. She was kissing him, pushing his breath away, forcing him to pant into her mouth. She seemed to struggle against him, fighting to get closer. Their noises were close too, so heavy between their skins that he heard the alien sound, the crunch of footsteps, as if it were a warning he had been expecting.

Still holding Stella, he opened his eyes as a slouching form disappeared around the corner of the house. He heard the whirring of an engine, saw the dim splash of headlights deep in the yard, listened for the distant rumble of the car falling into darkness. And still he held Stella Willis to him, as if his life depended on it.

Chapter Eleven

At night, when the house was hushed with breathing and the feathering of moth wings against the screens, James Earl lay awake.

He didn't see how his children could sleep so peacefully, dead themselves in sleep, when their mother had been gone only two weeks.

But they had gone to bed dry-eyed, and Anne said that in the daytime they asked for Mae only occasionally: Baby Earl when he stubbed his toe and held the bleeding hurt up to the wrong woman; Lissy more often, when she awoke to arms that weren't her mother's. Stella and William were working with him in the packhouse, thinking about God knows what as they went silently about their work, not crying or asking, not seeming to expect anything from him. He was grateful for that. He'd never given them much, and now he seemed to have even less to offer.

Yet he knew his life was taking on some kind of normality that he couldn't comprehend. He still wanted to grieve aloud as he had those first few days when his hurt had been like a knife wound—no, not like a slit that could seal itself and finally disappear, but more like a gunshot wound, irreparable, open to the air, and streaming his life blood. He didn't want his hurt to heal quickly because he was more afraid of guilt than of pain.

How could he have loved her and used her, had these children from her, and then forgotten so soon? That's what he thought in the daylight, when Silas would say, "Let's go in to dinner," and James Earl would start off toward his own house, forgetting—how could it be?—that Mae wasn't there.

But in the night he remembered. Coming in from the packhouse at twilight, he remembered because the coming darkness brought thoughts like goblins to haunt him, and he was afraid to be alone. What will I do? he would think, seeing his children around Anne's table. What will become of us?

Newton seemed to think things could stay the same, but James Earl knew better. Anne was having her baby soon; her back and legs ached from standing too much and from lifting Lissy. When the packhouse work was finished, Stella could take on the cooking and cleaning, even the washing if Anne would let her use the machines in her utility room. Soon Stella and William would be in school, and he would be doing whatever had to be done—more than likely digging potatoes, feeling the earth growing chill in his hands and his fingernails filthy with the rich soil of his home—now Mae's home, too. Newt thought it could be like that and so did James Earl in the daylight, but at night . . .

Now he washed under the shower spray in the dark because he couldn't stand to look at his body in the harsh light that made shadows as black and deep as a bottomless pit. He washed methodically, the soap slipping on his skin, unfelt because he intended not to feel, and all the time, as the hot spray splattered his skin, he was crying. He longed for Mae then, while their children, his life without her, slept and he was alone with a body that still needed her and didn't seem to know that she wasn't there in the bedroom, half-asleep and waiting.

Dried and naked, he went through Stella's room in the darkness and into the place where Mae should be and where now Lissy slept in the crib, her fingers in her mouth. He leaned over her and put his cool hand on her cheek. She seemed to have a fever, to be boiling beneath her skin with some raging disease. She was dying. Fear gripped him like the fire in her skin, and he wanted to scream but caught the cry in his throat, trying to gather his senses and convince himself of what he knew to be true. The baby was cool and sleeping. There was nothing to be afraid of.

He got into bed and pulled the sheet over his face. Looking at the underside of the sheet was like looking into a snow mound, and he thought suddenly of how long it had been since he'd seen snow. So long since he'd held a hard-packed ball in his hand and thrown it, watching it spin and then disintegrate on someone's back. Whose? Newton's. Yeah, he'd harassed Newton, who'd run, his short, fat legs stumbling in their heavy wrappings, tears and snow light blurring his eyes. Never running home toward Mama, but away, across a field, making himself easy prey in the frozen ridges and gulleys of the turned-up field. Didn't he know better?

Under the sheet, James Earl was crying. He thought at first that it was Newton he heard stumbling and running in his head, but then he knew it was his own noise and then Stella's voice drifting in over him, hovering in the snow that surrounded his head.

"Daddy," she was saying. "Oh, Daddy." She held back the sheet to look at his face in the half-dark. "Daddy." She put her hand on his cheek just as he'd touched Lissy, testing his feverishness.

He wanted to stop crying, felt the necessity of it for his child's sake, but the sobs came and he lay there, his body aching, trembling like a baby after a tantrum.

"Daddy," Stella said again and began to lift the covers. He was one of her children—had always been that—and she was coming to bring him comfort.

"No," he said hoarsely. "I ain't dressed."

Stella put the covers back against his chest and, without hesitating or thinking beyond loving him, lay down on top of the sheet beside him and took his hand, holding it in hers until he went to sleep.

Maggie Grover, proprietress of Grover's Department Store, saw them coming into church, James Earl in the lead holding Baby Earl by the hand, practically dragging him, and then the other boy, then Stella carrying Lissy, who ought to have been in the nursery downstairs. Maggie moved her head a little, not intending to make her beckoning obvious. James Earl saw the bobbing of her white straw hat, a new hat from the shine and style of it, and he turned into the pew where she sat alone like a sentry guarding their place.

She had, in fact, invited him to church in that biting tone of hers. Yesterday, after she'd rung up his purchases on the cash register and given the children each a penny box of Chiclets from the candy jar she kept on the counter, she'd said bluntly, "They ought to be going to church, don't you think, James Earl?"

James Earl had looked surprised, as if the thought were new to him, although Anne had tried to get them to church all summer; but Mae wouldn't go, and he wouldn't go without her. Now all that was changed. And Maggie's words and the half-embarrassed expression on her face when she heard her own reprimand had nothing to do with religion or what the children needed, but with Maggie Grover herself, proprietress of the store, middle-aged, single, a woman who sometime during the past weeks had given thought to him.

"Maybe we will," he said pleasantly. He felt strangely strong, newly masculine. Looking at her primness, her narrow fragility in a summer cotton shirt and skirt, he felt a surge of attractiveness in himself. It was a new feeling, one laid to rest when he'd married Mae, and now he realized that with her death it had been reborn. One spirit replaced another.

"Maybe we will," he repeated, this time boldly. "Kind of you to think of us, Maggie."

"Just you think about it," Maggie said, reddening under his powerful stare. She put her hand to her throat, covering her Adam's apple in a nervous gesture she'd fought for years. Mama used to say she had a neck like a goose, just one of the painfully true things Mama used to say.

"Thank Miss Maggie for the gum," James Earl had said to the children, and they'd murmured thank-you's, staring at her as if she were an oddity.

Now they sat down the pew from her with James Earl closest, only room enough for a child between them, and he had set Baby Earl down there and pulled William closer to him, so they were all close together although the church was roasting hot and other people were spreading out, trying to get cool. Anne and Newton entered from the door next to the pulpit, coming from their Sunday school class, and James Earl gave them an embarrassed grin and the children waved shyly, grateful for familiar faces. The children were wearing their funeral clothes and looked stiff and grown, like very old people. Anne and Newton passed them quickly and went to find seats of their own, while Maggie Grover held a bulletin in her gloved, perspiring hand and prayed that her neck wasn't growing red under the imagined stares behind her.

What had she been thinking of, she wondered, to say such a thing to James Earl when it was none of her business whether they came to church or not? Of course, it was for the children's sake, she remembered. She tried to decipher her motives more carefully so that she could join in the preacher's sermon and the hymns and prayers unchallenged by her own private thoughts. But James Earl Willis, a widower—a man—was too close, and she couldn't think beyond that fact—that he was a man and that she, deep through the unbroken thread of her femininity, was a woman.

After the service, James Earl stood with Baby Earl pulling at his pants' leg and Lissy squirming in his arms next to Maggie on the church porch. The six of them stood in the shade of the roof away from the noon sun and seemed to be hesitating there as if they expected something to happen and were waiting to see how it would affect them. James Earl shifted Lissy's weight and saw for the first time that they were with him—his four children and a woman—all he needed in his life if he could stay and work his little bit of land.

The woman stood silently, wondering what to do next. It seemed to her that her life had changed, that sitting next to James Earl Willis in church this once had altered her future so that she was dependent on him. She waited.

For more than two months she'd been watching him, from the moment he'd parked that terrible old station wagon under George's shelter and tumbled out. She'd seen him coming into town with Newton and Silas, the three of them looking like mischievous boys let out of a church school for the afternoon. She'd seen the girl, Stella, in Rodney Biggers' car, seen Mae once walking alone, sneaking up the street in broad daylight like she wished it were night and she could disappear into it. And of course, she'd seen Mae dead.

She'd stood a long time, longer than she should have, and looked at the face, worn-out and heavily made-up, with those silly finger waves Jean Biggers was still defending to anybody who'd give her the time of day. She had wanted to memorize the face— to remember it—in the specific way that someone studies the movements of a person they intend to impersonate. Even then, she was conscious of what newly grew in the back of her head—a flower of her future with James Earl Willis—where loneliness had long ago settled like a gigantic, rooted weed.

Looking at Mae's face, she'd wondered how it could have been that he'd married that woman who could never have been pretty, when he'd always been such a handsome boy, full of jokes and good times. She remembered James Earl well, remembered him in the store trying on boots and things when he was a boy and she not so much older than he but already helping Papa in the store because there was no one else to do it. And besides, what else did she have, even then?

She had studied Mae's face, aware that she could, if luck were with her, take her place in James Earl's bed in her big old house where she lived alone with too much emptiness. She had a great deal to offer a man like him—money, a house and business, the mothering of his children, comfort in his loneliness, a body eager to be given.

Now on the church porch, she summoned a courage that seemed to be fleeting and said to him, "Alice, who cooks for me, she'll have plenty of dinner if you want to bring the children and come on over to the house." She hesitated and slid her tongue lightly across her upper lip. "It would give Newton and Anne a rest."

James Earl heard her and knew what she was saying better than she did. He grinned sheepishly into the sunlight. "Kind of you, Maggie," he said. "We'd like that."

He'd never felt such boyish pride. Never had he been so sure of the course before him or the way to handle her. Charm, hidden in years of indecision and drudgery, edged his voice, and he tasted it like the memory of a delicious meal. He took Maggie's arm with his free hand and, shaking Baby Earl loose, marched with his brood down the steps, nodding and smiling until he reached Newton.

There he stopped and said close to his brother's face, "We're going down to Miss Maggie Grover's house for some dinner," and winked. By God, he winked without meaning to.

And then they went past Newton and Anne, down the street toward Maggie's unkempt, rambling house, leaving the station wagon in front of the church and every head on the church lawn turned in their direction.

After dinner, where the children had shown off the table manners learned from Anne and where James Earl had eaten heartily without the queasy stomach that should accompany the beginning of a courtship, they went out on the front porch and sat down in the matching rockers that had belonged to Maggie's mother and father.

The sun was coming in at them, and Lissy lay down on the glider that was edged with sunlight and went to sleep without a word, her hand across her mouth, but without her thumb pushed against her gums. She seemed especially content and James Earl sighed, letting the sound come out evenly, showing his contentment too, while the older children raced into the side yard where an ancient swing hung from an oak tree.

James Earl could see them without turning his head—Stella's dark dress hiding her in the tree's shadow except for the flicker of arms, legs, and golden hair when she rose behind the swing that carried Baby Earl and, grabbing ahold, lifted herself into the air for a moment like an angel and then dropped back with a thump to the grass while Baby Earl sailed up and out, an angel himself, with the worn, corded wings of Maggie Grover's swing.

"That was yours, wasn't it?" he asked. "I remember coming by here years ago and swinging in that swing. I guess everybody in town's sat in that swing some time or other."

"Yes," Maggie said, looking out at the children. "But not anymore. Children don't come by, although I get a new rope every few years just in case. People ride too much. Have you noticed that, James Earl? People come to the store and park right there in front and don't walk more than ten steps. We used to walk, though, everywhere we went because Papa didn't get out the car except in bad weather and for real trips, like to Lawrence." She stopped abruptly. It's wrong to tell him about the past, she thought. It'll only remind us both of things best forgotten.

But the idea had caught on in James Earl's head, and he had words for it. "Do you remember, Maggie, when the bank building was painted brick red, and almost before the paint was dry, somebody wrote on it with white paint? 'So long, it's been good to know you,' it said. That was Bobby Turner and me. That was just days before I went to Texas, and Bobby and me wrote that. A childish prank is what it was," he explained, suddenly wary about her understanding him.

Maggie was smiling. "Bobby Turner confessed," she recalled. "But he didn't say you were with him. You were gone by then, anyhow, but the sheriff—it was Tyler then—he made Bobby go out there and paint over it in broad daylight in front of the whole town and then some."

"I worried about it," James Earl said, still distrustful of her reaction. "But it was a thing like boys will do. Earl and William'll probably do something like that someday."

The boys were flying in the swing, William standing and Baby Earl crouched between his legs. It looked dangerous when the rope jumped in William's hands.

"Stella!" James Earl called in a voice that carried across the yard but didn't startle the sleeping Lissy. "Y'all be careful!"

"I'm watching out, Daddy!" she called back, her voice full of careless laughter.

"My whole life has been in this town, in this house," Maggie said quickly as if she had to get the words out before the tears started. She was looking out at the children, the boys flung in the air outside the foliage of the oak, their bodies thin and defenseless against the blue and white sky.

"It's as good a place as any," James Earl said, not looking at her. He didn't want to see her face.

"Papa died ten years ago, and of course you remember we'd been without Mama for years before that. Ten years I've been alone in this house, and at the store, too, because who can you trust, James Earl? Who can you depend on?" Maggie sniffed into a tissue that had been crumpled in her fist since dinner.

"You're a nice-looking woman, Maggie," James Earl said as lightly as he could. "You should of gotten married, found a man to take care of things for you."

"Nobody asked me," Maggie blew her nose. "Not that I didn't get courted some, but you see, Papa didn't want me to move away. I was all he had and by the time he died, I was thirty—I'm forty years old, James Earl—and nobody asked me."

Lissy was stirring and James Earl moved quickly to keep her from falling off the glider. She awoke in his arms and put her face, wet from sweat and saliva, against his chest.

"I guess I better get these kids on home," he said. "Thank you for the dinner, Maggie. We appreciate it."

"I'm glad you came," Maggie said. Her face was red and dry. She stood up and leaned against the porch railing.

"Stella!" James Earl called. "Come on. We got to get going!" He turned back to Maggie and held Lissy between them. "I'd like to come by sometime, Maggie, if you don't mind. Sometimes I get sorta lonesome now."

"You come by anytime," Maggie said. She was beginning to smile. "We remember each other, James Earl," she said boldly, "if that matters any."

The children were waiting on the walk, and James Earl joined them with Lissy holding onto his neck. Together they went down the street and out of her sight to the rumbling old car that had brought them this far.

Chapter Twelve

Toby knew something was going to happen. Kissing Stella had been an act of finality akin to old Mrs. Willis' suicide or even Mae's death. He knew it could create a chain of events that would hurt him, but while he was kissing her and all through the night, he didn't really care.

At home in his bed, he lay in the warm darkness remembering Stella's face, the touch of her hand on his shirt, her mouth pressed against his. Thinking about Stella made his groin ache and he reached down in the darkness to touch himself.

He could see his body against the white sheet, his legs spread, his thighs still thin but becoming fleeced with coarse, curling hair. The part of his body covered by his shorts seemed to melt into the sheet, but his penis pushed hard against the fabric. His chest was brown, with the ribs jutting out as he breathed.

His arms lay one stretched out, a dark, thin line, the other against his side, bringing his hand to the pain.

He wouldn't panic. He held back the fear that rushed him like a fever and turned into the pillow, destroying his perfect form on the white sheet, trying to make himself invisible.

On Saturday they found him in the pool hall. He was standing against the wall watching the players shoot, making a shadow of himself, when he felt the rush of steamy, sunlit air and saw two boys come in and start toward him, not really menacing, but smiling as if they had won the door prize and he was it. Toby didn't know their names, but he knew they were much older than he was and used the gym equipment at school. They introduced themselves.

"I'm George. This is Lucien. And you're Toby Brown," one of them said, latching his thumbs into his front belt loops.

"We're friends of Rodney Biggers," Lucien said, chuckling. He had been drinking beer, and the smell lay in the cool, smoky air between them. "Rodney don't come in places like this," Lucien said. He laughed with startling loudness, as if someone had just tickled him.

"Rodney ain't worth two cents," George said.

"Sure he is. One thing Rodney's got is money."

The boys punched at each other laughing.

Toby wished they'd get on with it. "This ain't no party," he muttered finally while the boys laughed.

"You damn right it ain't," Lucien said, his laughter stopping as abruptly as it had begun. "Rodney wants you to come with us. He says you ain't a nice boy. In fact, he says you put your trashy hands on his girl. He says you come with us."

The hollow noise of the pool balls breaking drifted across the room. The men playing pool didn't look up. Most of them had a day's wages on their game.

"All right," Toby said.

He had planned to fight. Knowing this or something like it would happen, he had spent the week planning strategy, thinking about escapes or even killing someone. But now he was weaponless, brainless, his mind telling him over and over the one thing he knew to be true: they could kill him if they wanted to.

Outside, the sunlight made him blink, and he thought for a second how light could be a destructive thing. He thought of Stella's hair, a sun cap on her head, then of the lightning that had charred the chain.

Night is better, he thought, climbing into the waiting car. He closed his eyes, finding darkness and feeling the car move under him as Rodney Biggers turned the Impala out of a no-parking zone and onto the back road to Lawrence.

Nobody called the sheriff. The people who found him, a black couple coming down the edge of the woods where their still was hidden, didn't want the law coming around. Besides, it wouldn't have done any good.

In the boy's pants' pocket they found a plastic, stitch-sided wallet with his name in it. They laid him on the kitchen table and while the wife slit his shirt and tried to wash the dirt and blood off his face and chest, the man went to the nearest white house where he used the telephone, his thick, calloused fingers barely catching in the holes as he dialed. He knew to call the minister.

By the time the man arrived, swirling dust under his car up the narrow path, Toby was coming to. His chest and arms hurt so he couldn't breathe deeply and he couldn't talk. When he swallowed, pain cut into his throat and his saliva made him retch. His pulse pounded in his face and his lips showed the imprint of his teeth in marks that continued to bleed even though the woman wiped at them gently, trying not to hurt him.

"It's Silas Brown's boy," he heard the man saying to the preacher. "Somebody near beat him to death."

When the man neared the table, Toby tried to get up, but his body hurt too much for him to move and he fell back on the pillow the woman had shoved under his head.

"Don't move, son," the preacher said. He was wearing a suit with a vest and a gold chain looped across his round middle. Toby watched the chain flickering in the light.

"I don't think nothin's broken," the woman said. "Maybe some cracked ribs. Maybe not. I reckon he ought to see the doctor, though." She sounded weary with Toby, wanting him off her table so she could get on with supper.

"No," Toby whispered. "Home. Newton Willis."

"That might be the best thing," the man said to the preacher. "Mr. Willis oughta decide about this thing."

"Help me get him in the car," the preacher said after silent deliberation.

The man picked Toby up like a baby and carried him to the car. The wooly fabric of the car seat itched his skin, but he couldn't complain. Don't talk, he thought. Don't think. Don't do anything . . .

The car bumped down the path and turned onto the highway where the riding was smoother. Toby felt himself sailing. The windows were down, and the breeze of coming night was cool around him.

I'm alive, he thought after a while. I'm alive. He closed his eyes, trying to see in his mind's eye one more day in his life, but he couldn't. Tears ran from the corners of his eyes along the edge of his dirty hair to his ears, stinging his raw cheeks, and his mind was as blank as the empty sky before the coming of day.

On the second day, he started running a fever. Anne leaned over him, her bulging stomach close to his bruised face, and put her hand on his forehead.

"Fever," she said to his mother, Synora, who stood across the cot from her in the kitchen of the big house. She was holding a mason jar of her special salve. It was all Toby could smell. His face was smeared yellow with it, and it stung his nostrils and watered his eyes. Or was he crying? He couldn't tell.

Sometimes he thought tears just came for no reason or because his body was weeping for itself. Only once had he consciously cried since the afternoon in the preacher's car. That was yesterday when Anne let Stella into the kitchen for a minute, and he opened his eyes a little to see her.

She was a blur of white and silver, a streak of lightning above his head. He wanted to see her clearly, to remember in case something worse happened. He closed his eyes to blink away the tears, but the blur wouldn't focus. Even her voice was distant, detached, alien.

"Stella," he whispered, wanting to stop her anxious chatter.

"Don't talk," a voice said back to him. "Anne won't let me stay if you talk."

So suddenly there were rules again. Don't talk, don't move, don't touch.

"Rodney did this," the voice said. "I know he's responsible."

The voice seemed angry, and Toby knew part of the anger was directed at him.

"I know you won't tell," she was saying. "Because that would mean telling why he did it. He saw us, didn't he? Don't say anything. I thought I heard a car that night, but I didn't suspect it to be Rodney. Why should I? I didn't have plans to go anywhere with him that night. It was the day of Mama's funeral, wasn't it? Well, he shouldn't of been there." She sighed impatiently. Whispering didn't suit her anger.

"I could kill the bastard with my bare hands," she said. "I would, too, except that people would know, Toby. We can't let that happen. I mean, Newton and Anne, what would they think?"

The voice stopped abruptly, as if someone had clamped a hand over her mouth, but he knew she'd stopped talking of her own accord. She was gone.

He wanted to answer her, to have her understand that he wasn't ashamed, but he knew already that what he felt didn't matter. Stella was regretful, ashamed. All his pain focused on that bit of vulnerability. She was right to be ashamed, but he hated her for it. He began to cry, not just tears but deep sobs in his chest that wrenched his body and left him exhausted.

"He's delirious," he heard Anne saying. "Newton, if he's not better tomorrow, we'll have to take him to the hospital."

Tomorrow came out of the darkness behind Toby's squinting eyelids, and Anne was putting a thermometer between his swollen lips.

"Don't bite down, honey," she said. "I'll hold it for you. It's under your tongue, isn't it? Won't tell you a thing if it isn't."

The only place for people without insurance in the hospital was a ten-bed ward with portable screens between the patients. Newton signed the financial guarantee, and a black orderly wheeled Toby into the room and lifted him onto a bed which was very hard and high, with slick cold sheets. The orderly put a thin blanket over him, and instantly Toby felt warm.

After a long time, the doctor came. He was a big man who had once removed a nail from Toby's foot, and he held Toby's limp hand while talking to Anne and Newton. "Pulse and blood pressure okay. His skin ruptures seem to be doing all right." He smiled at Anne. "You've been doing a good job."

"But the fever," Anne said anxiously.

"Well, he's pretty badly battered up. Probably needs some ribs taped. We'll make x-rays. The fever is from a low-grade infection. This many skin abrasions generally need an antibiotic. You'll be all right, son," the doctor said, patting Toby's hand.

Toby felt them moving away. His eyes closed against the room's glare, and he listened to the silence, a cough across the room, a plastic mattress cover crackling as a body shifted.

"Who the hell did that to him?" he heard the doctor asking.

"I don't know," Newton answered. "I wish to God I did."

"Does it matter?" Anne asked. "Just get him well. He's such a good boy."

No, I'm not, Toby thought, his battered chest paining with every breath, and I don't ever want anybody to know.

Chapter Thirteen

Maggie Grover could imagine James Earl in the store. While her lucid, businesslike mind told her he knew nothing about dry goods and probably not much more about hardware, her imagination, having lain dormant for so many years, spun an elaborate picture of him behind the counter greeting customers and in the stockroom with the salesmen ordering nails and roto-tillers and castiron frying pans.

She'd keep the dry goods if he couldn't manage it all right away. She could order shoes, dresses, material, without even looking at the samples. Her customers weren't influenced by fashion any more than she was. Besides, they wore what she had to sell whatever it was and didn't complain either, except when the price crept up. Lately, that was happening a lot too often.

Maggie was a wealthy woman, and yet the thought had never entered her head that she could give up the store, which gave her fierce headaches and fits of exhaustion at the end of the day, leaving her lifeless, unable to eat or think. The store kept making money even with inflation, but profit meant increasing her tithe and sometimes selling a little cheaper than anyone else could afford to. She had to take care of herself, though. Until James Earl came, she'd spent considerable time contemplating her final years, and she intended to have enough money for the best nursing home in the county, if it came to that. And it would, because there was no one in her family to take on the burden of her aging.

She'd taken care of her mama when she was barely out of her teens, racing from the store where Papa needed her to the house where Mama lay as still and white as the ghost she soon became. She had had a heart attack and was afraid to move, even after the doctor had said a little exercise might be the best thing.

"He's trying to kill me," her mama would say about the doctor. "He don't want to bother with coming around here twice a week listening to this mess inside my poor chest, so he's trying to get me up so I can fall dead."

She died anyway, lying there trying not to let her heart beat too much, resenting all of them, saving herself as best she could because she wanted to live to see Maggie married and with children; while Maggie, lifting the weakening frame and toting dinner trays and bedpans, made a haggard slave of herself between the store and the house.

What did money matter when it meant living and dying like her parents had? she thought. They seemed to have existed just because living was there to do, not because there was any joy in it.

Maggie had felt that way, too, but now there was joy in the form of James Earl Willis. One whole day hadn't passed since that Sunday dinner before there he was, leaning across her counter like he owned the place, saying, "Maggie, where you keep the bandages, thermometers, and the like?" He sounded worried and angry at something, but also familiar, like he could let her know how he was feeling.

She went silently to the shelf where she kept the meager selection of medical supplies. "What's the matter?" she asked while she was putting gauze, tape, and a thermometer in front of him.

"It's Toby Brown. Somebody near killed him Saturday night. Some colored folks found him and brought him home. Yesterday when we got home, Synora had brought him up to Anne's house, she was so worried. Now Anne's got him in the kitchen up there trying to bandage him up. We think he's running a fever though, so he'll more than likely end up in Lawrence in the hospital."

"Why would anybody do that?" Maggie asked.

"I don't know," James Earl said. "But goddamn whoever it was. I'll kill 'em if I ever get my hands on 'em."

Maggie felt dizzy. The power in his voice touched her brain and sent her spinning. Already she loved his rage. She could imagine him killing the culprit, strangling him with the giant hands that now thumped the counter in heavy, blunt fists. Strangely, the picture didn't frighten her at all, but spread, hot and smoldering, inside her skin.

"I hope he'll be all right," she whispered. Her voice seemed lost inside her body. Her fingers clutched the thermometer casing until her hand was damp.

"I reckon he will." James Earl's anger was subsiding, and he looked at her. "I meant what I said about coming to see you, Maggie," he said gently. "I could come one night this week—Wednesday, if that's convenient."

She had circle meeting. Someday he would know that every other Wednesday night for the past twenty years she'd sat in a circle of women and heard prayers and programs about missions over-seas and at home and eaten a light dessert because everybody else was dieting. Some day he would know that, but not yet. "Wednesday would be fine," she said. "Could you come for supper?"

"That's kind of you, Maggie, but I'd better be seeing to the children since Anne's so busy with Toby. I could come around eight, though." He col-lected his purchases and the money fell into her hand.

She had wanted to say, "Don't pay. Everything here is yours; it belongs to you." But she couldn't, and so she made change and dropped the coins into his open palm. "Here, wait," she had said as he was going out the door, "Take these to the children." It was a bag of bite-size chocolate bars, the first thing her hand had touched.

"Why, thank you, Maggie," he said. He was smil-ing. The smile came just for her, and she smiled back.

"I'll see you on Wednesday," she said.

"On Wednesday."

She thought Wednesday would never come, with two hot August nights between that bothered her sleep and made her stomach quiver when she tried to swallow. She forced herself to eat. She was too thin already. She couldn't come to James Earl as gaunt and deathlike as Mae had been.

In the store, her mood shifted from impatience to euphoria, from despair that she knew nothing about fashion and therefore had no new dress to wear, to glee that she could offer him the house, the pride of the town when he was a boy. He would remember that. The furniture was all the same; the curtains newer but the same elaborate style her mother had liked; the kitchen appliances and bathroom fixtures were serviceable relics. The house was old, but it had quality, and James Earl hadn't seemed to think it looked shabby on Sunday. In the evening light, Maggie knew the house would have the aura of a sumptuous past that would attract him.

Now she stood at the door watching him come up the porch. Alice had already gone home after setting out the sherry bottle on a tray and covering sliced pound cake with plastic wrap. They would be alone.

"James Earl." She led him into the parlor, feeling that this time she was truly leading him into her life. Without the buffer of the children, she felt both frightened and relieved that they were finally beginning this adventure of knowing each other again. He sat in her father's chair, not on it as her father had, but slouched inside it comfortably as if, she thought, the chair were his already. She sat on the end of the sofa closest to him, a table and a lamp between them. The lamplight lay on her arms and on his legs. They were silent, immobile.

"How is Toby?" she asked finally.

"In the hospital. The doctor says he'll be okay." James Earl sighed and tapped his fingers on the armrest.

He's bored, she thought. Already I'm losing him. "And Stella?" she asked in desperation, remembering how he'd seemed to love the girl more openly than the other children.

"She's upset about Toby, I reckon. Been moping

around. Anne let her see him one time, and the whole rest of the day she didn't say a word. That ain't like Stella. She's got spunk and a word for anything." He was relaxing. The strain of loneliness loosened gently in him like violin strings searching cleaner harmony.

"There's something I want to say to you, Maggie," he said so quickly she felt her breath leaving in one gigantic gasp. "It's about Mae—and, well, about you and me. Mae's been gone less than two months—it's more like one month, I guess—but for me, it's been years. I feel years of loneliness in me, Maggie, years of being sad and of pretending I know what to do with the children—with my life, for that matter.

"I haven't been able to figure things out very well yet. All those years we were on the road, I didn't have to think beyond getting the car to run and having us a place to sleep at night. But since I've come home, things are getting complicated, like there's more to deal with in a man's life than I thought.

"And here you are, Maggie, complicating things more. Without meaning to, of course, and I mean to tell you, I'm grateful for your kindness to me and the children. The truth is, Maggie, I'm wanting to court you. In my mind I can even see us getting married someday. I wanted to tell you that, so we'd understand each other right off. You might not want any part of me and my troubles, and if you don't, you'd best be blunt about it and say so, because otherwise, I intend to court you, Maggie, as best I can."

She was certain her heart had stopped beating. The lamplight began to shimmer like sunlight on waves, and she shut her eyes against the glare, feeling herself float off on a tremendous curl that could lift her forever if she let it.

"James Earl," she said without opening her eyes, "there's sherry on the tray over there. Let's have some."

He put the stemmed goblet in her hand, and she gripped it as delicately as she could, feeling his closeness because James Earl had sat down on the sofa next to her, their thighs touching. She sipped the sherry. It was sticky and hot, like sorghum. The liquid oozed down her throat and then up into her head.

"I won't stand in the way of your courting me, James Earl," she said slowly, her tongue thick with wine. "And as for marriage, that will come if it will. I told you already nobody ever asked me. You know my secrets, James Earl, and I'm willing to trust you to handle them with care. I want to trust you."

"You can, Maggie." He put his hand on her knee. Through the softness of her summer dress, the warmth of his flesh crept into her and she lay her own hand over his, pressing gently, molding his hand under hers.

"I know nothing about love," she said after awhile. "No, that's not true. I think I know a great deal about love, but nothing about sex. Maybe I'm too old."

"And maybe," James Earl said, "when we're young we know too much about sex and too little about love."

Maggie turned to him, her eyes shining with the wine, and put her hands on his face tentatively, not as if she were afraid, but more as if wanting to savor the moment and memory of him. "That was a lovely thing to say."

Her fingers reached his mouth, and he kissed them gently, parting his lips in her palm, then curling her fingers so her knuckles were against his mouth and he breathed on her hand.

"I never thought I'd have children, even someone else's. I'd given up on ever being wanted. And now there's a chance for there to be people in this house, children in it who can grow up and come back to it. This house has been needing that for such a long time, and so have I."

Drained of emotions, stripped defenseless of their secret selves, they leaned into each other's arms and stayed there, as still as the shadows in the silent room and the ghosts that had been laid to rest in both of them.

Chapter Fourteen

Rodney Biggers sat on Stella's front porch while the sweat ran down his back and collected in a soggy stripe above his belt. He was wearing new clothes, yellow slacks the color of lemon ice cream and a white shirt with a yellow flower design on it. He had thought new clothes might give him courage because he was afraid of this initial meeting with Stella. All week he'd worried about it, knowing he couldn't avoid running into her, wondering when his mother was going to notice his staying home at night, wishing he could be with Stella just like before because he missed her.

Rodney had a fundamental belief in punishment that had never been disproven. Because the terrible thing that had happened to Toby Brown was his responsibility, he had half expected an overt, divine punishment—an automobile wreck that killed his parents, the house burning down. Since no ominous signs of disaster had appeared, he now contemplated a more subtle kind of retribution: Stella would tell on him.

But Rodney hadn't come to shut her up. After all, he still envisioned walking her to the soda shop after school and driving her home in the car while Toby took the bus. Rodney knew he wouldn't be alone, wondering what to do with himself, if he had Stella Willis.

With Toby in the hospital, Rodney had a vague sense of how impossible his dream was. He was scared. He hadn't intended for Lucien and George to hurt Toby so bad. A warning was what he'd intended, but once those guys had started getting in licks, he couldn't stop them until Toby was unconscious on the ground, as soft as a down pillow. They'd hit him until it wasn't fun anymore, and there was nothing Rodney could do but leave him there and drive the boys back into town. He paid them five dollars, too. Five dollars was all it took to hire what could have amounted to a killing.

Rodney pressed his palms into the splintered arms of the weather-beaten chair. He wished Stella would come out so he could get this talk over with, although he didn't know exactly what he was going to say to her. He'd been planning to pretend that he didn't know a thing about Toby, but while waiting for Stella, he realized that she probably knew he was the cause of it and would throw it in his face like a dirty dishrag. He knew she could splatter him with anger and disgust and hatefulness if she wanted to.

The screen door swung open, and she was standing there dressed up in that blue dress, looking like she'd just arrived from heaven. Rodney felt his eyes misting over, blurring with sweat and tears at the sight of her.

"Daddy said you were out here," she said wearily and sat down on the glider without looking at him. She stared out at the sky, which was hazy with heat and dust. "I couldn't believe my ears." Her voice seemed to travel on the heat very slowly.

Rodney sucked in his breath and gripped the arms of the chair. He was sitting in a puddle of sweat, and his shorts and shirt stuck to him. "I've been planning to come ever since your mama died," he began.

"You came, Rodney. Don't you lie to me on top of everything else you've done." Stella's voice was as cold as the waves of sweat on his skin and he shuddered. He had lost her.

"Toby's in the hospital. Newton took me to see him. He looks better now. At least he's not as swollen. His face was so hurt, Rodney. All week I've been thinking he won't look the same ever again, so when I saw him today at the hospital I just wanted to cry with relief. He's going to look the same. But you're always going to look different to me, no matter how fancy your clothes get or how many new cars you drive. You're gonna look like a skunk, Rodney, because what you did to Toby is so stinking and hateful and yellow that I'll remember it every time I look at you."

Rodney was crying. Tears mixed with perspiration around his eyes and stung him. "I didn't mean for it to be so bad," he sobbed, still sitting straight in the chair. "I didn't want anything but for him to leave you alone."

"I'm not telling anybody—not even Daddy or

Newt," Stella said. "Neither is Toby. But I'll never forget. Not ever. I don't ever want you coming here again."

Her voice wasn't like he'd ever heard it before. There was calmness in it and purpose and such a lack of regret that Rodney felt as if the past month with her had been a dream only he had lived through. He didn't move.

"Just get off this porch, Rodney Biggers," she was saying. "You just stay off my property."

Rodney stumbled off the porch and into the car. The rasping engine closed in around him. Protected by his seatbelt, the cool drone of the air conditioner, the soothing voice of a disc jockey wishing him a happy day, he pulled out onto the road, while Stella sat with folded hands as if she were in a church pew having her life explained to her.

When Toby came home from the hospital, Stella was waiting for him on Synora's front porch.

"They're here!" she cried when the car carrying Newt, Silas, and Toby started up the road. She could hear Synora bustling in the kitchen, finishing a meal that had taken all morning to cook.

"Everything's ready," Synora said, coming to the screen door and looking out at her.

"Here they are!" Stella jumped off the porch as the dust settled and Toby crawled out of the back seat. He looked like a ghost, much whiter and thinner than he'd seemed in the hospital, where Stella had expected him to look sick. Now she wanted him to be the old Toby.

He came slowly up the steps without waiting for

Silas to help him and sat down on the first chair he came to.

"He's tired out," Synora said worriedly. "Just riding home's wore him down."

"That's to be expected, Synora," Silas said. "The doctor said you feed him good and he'll be the same old Toby in a few days."

"Well, dinner's ready," she said and touched her son's shoulder.

"You staying around?" Toby asked Stella.

"Your mama invited me, if that's all right with you."

"Yeah." He smiled, but his eyes were still dull. "I've been missing you."

"Me, too."

"You all come eat," Synora urged, wanting the day to fit her expectations.

"I got to get my wind back, Mama," Toby said. "You and Daddy go ahead. We're coming in a minute."

"I was so scared when you went to the hospital," Stella said when Synora and Silas had gone inside. "Even that day I went to see you and I could see you were all right, I was still so scared. It was deep inside where I think my heart must be, and it was breaking because you were so sick and I was the cause of it."

"No, Stella."

"Rodney came. He had the nerve to drive right out here and sit on my front porch like nothing had happened. I told him I didn't want to see him ever again. And that's the truth, Toby."

"You all come on and eat!" Synora called.

"We're spoiling your mama's celebration," Stella said. "She made a cake and all, just like a party."

Toby stood up, stumbling a little, and Stella caught his arm. He leaned against her for a moment, wishing he had all the strength loving her took.

"We can try to be friends," he said finally. "Even if you change your mind about Rodney Biggers, we can try."

James Earl's world moved in slow motion. Although August was ending, he felt the days lengthening, had time on his hands, and the future seemed to move tediously, just outside his grasp. Stella and William were in school, riding the bus which stopped for Toby and them in front of Newton's house each morning. He could hear them even before he was up; Stella already in the kitchen fixing sandwiches for the lunch boxes Anne had supplied, coaxing William against dawdling, laughing, bitching sometimes when her patience wore thin.

Stella pushed time away, teased it, grabbed it back. The days were all good for her now that Toby was well, and she fluttered about, clucking at Baby Earl and Lissy, telling James Earl what needed doing around the house, poring over the schoolbooks that she carried tightly against her chest as if they might somehow escape her grasp.

James Earl wanted to grab life as Stella had, and yet old worries bogged him down so that sometimes he regretted having come home at all. If they were still on the road, he would think, Mae would be alive, they'd be moving, time wouldn't be bothering him; only the weather and how many days they could manage to stay in one place. Mae never could stand more than a week in one place.

But here they were, stationary, and he the worse for it because his mind worked anxiously on insolvable problems like Maggie Grover. He didn't know what had gotten into him, talking to her like he had, although every time he went there he liked her better and felt more comfortable. Sitting evenings in her parlor and once in her old-timey kitchen that reminded him of his mama's, he felt alive and awake, fearless. He wanted to hurry up and marry her if he was going to.

Now that he knew her better, he believed he was beginning to love her. She assured him of permanence and comfort at least. Oh, hell, it was more than that. Already he loved her, even knowing that love was sometimes painful—you lose people and you hurt and you think the hurt will never stop, and sometimes it doesn't.

He'd seen Maggie Grover six times in three weeks. He would have been there every night if he could have gotten away without Anne and Newton knowing where he was going. He hadn't told them yet, knowing they would think it was too soon for him to be courting anybody, even Maggie Grover. He knew Anne's face would betray her when she was wondering what the town would think. Anne would be even more concerned about that than Maggie was, and he had to admit that Maggie brought the subject up too frequently to suit him, always protesting that she didn't care a whit what people thought and then adding a "but" that told him they shouldn't go out for supper yet or to the movies. They hadn't even sat in church together since that first Sunday.

But last night he'd tried to straighten the situation out a little. At least he could talk to Maggie; she seemed to grasp his meaning better than Mae had, as if their sharing of roots gave Maggie a special understanding of him.

He was kissing her good night—they were to the stage where he kissed her at the front door—"coming and going" he joked to her—and while she was still in his arms, he had said, "I want to marry you, Maggie, as soon as it's fitting."

She had moved back a little to collect herself, balancing against the hall table. He could see the back of her head, her shoulders down to her waist, in the mirror above the table. The back of her summer print dress was wrinkled, and James Earl was struck by the thought that where she couldn't see, the other side of herself, she wasn't prim—but somehow careless and unprotected. He felt he could see right through her at that moment, could set her aquiver with his hands, touch her vulnerability so softly that she would never know what easy prey she was. But he was still, waiting to let his words work on her.

"I want to marry you too," Maggie said softly. "Seems like I've been waiting a long time."

"Anne's having the baby in late September. We could get married after that."

"I just don't know, James," she said. "It's really very soon."

"And you care about that?" he asked, unable to resist touching her any longer. Once she was in his arms again he knew he would have his way. He put his hands on her shoulders, caressed her neck with his fingers, then cupped her face in his hands.

She was trembling. He knew he could do anything he wanted. Power pressed into his muscles, and he had to resist pulling her roughly against his chest.

"Folks here have never had reason to talk about me. I guess it's about time they did."

"Early October, then," James Earl said with his face close to hers.

"Early October," she nodded.

"Show me where you live, Maggie," he whispered.

There was no passage more secret than that, no place better hidden, but she took his hand and led him softly up the wide steps into the hall dimly lit with frosted sconces, past the room where her mother had died, the closed dusty sewing room, the useless nursery, into the space where, amidst the clutter of her child life, the doilies and sachets, photographs and heavy scrolled furniture, she was truly herself.

There was no reason for words between them now. The conversation of courtship seemed somehow over and the business of their lives together had not yet begun. It seemed as though these hours were the void they had to fill to reach the real world of the store, the town, the children.

At first, James Earl felt himself the intruder. Then he saw in Maggie's silent face the beginning of her welcome, a softening blush in her cheeks that told him she was more sure than he. This would be their room, their bed. In Maggie's face, James Earl saw her willingness to share it with him.

The bed was high and wonderfully clean, with a faint smell of bath powder in it. The smell alone was intoxicating, but soon James Earl felt heady with the pleasure of loving a woman who responded out of her own happiness. Already he had begun to love her strength, the resilience that let her abandon the bitterness she once harbored in her lonely past; now he loved her tenderness as well.

And Maggie, knowing the tangibleness of James Earl for the first time, held him close against herself until she felt her arms and heart would break with loving him.

So now he must tell Newton and Anne. Committed, he must face the discord his family could bring to his new harmony. Today, he thought. Then tonight I'll tell Stella, because she must know everything I feel as honestly as I can tell her.

"I'm courting Maggie Grover," he said to Stella later that night, after he'd endured Anne's silent stare and Newton's embarrassed back-slapping. The other children were in bed, and he was getting ready to go out.

"But she's old, Daddy," Stella said, looking up from her book. "She's older than you are."

"I know that, honey, but we've known each other since we were children and I like being with her. We're good friends."

"But courting means more than that, doesn't it? You're dating her." There was a hint of accusation in her voice.

"I go by her house to see her, that's all," James Earl lied. "That's not really dating, is it?"

"You still miss Mama a lot, don't you?" Stella closed her book.

The question seemed to be more empathy than accusation, and James Earl struggled to find an honest answer. "Yes, I miss her," he said. "Don't you?"

"Yes, but it's different. Like that night you were crying, and there wasn't a soul that could help you. I know I'm not the same as Mama. I know that."

"Then you'd understand if I wanted to marry

Maggie someday. She's got that big old house, so big we could just about get lost in it. She's got the store. I wouldn't mind working in a store if it meant having things for you children—for myself, too. Maggie could help bring up William and Earl and Lissy. They need a woman, and we can't expect Anne to take care of us forever."

"I can bring them up. You and me together can do it," Stella said.

"You wouldn't like doing that all the time, Stella. Soon enough you'll have friends at school and you'll be wanting to hang around at the soda shop and go places."

"But this is our house," Stella argued. "We can stay here as long as we want to."

James Earl felt suddenly tired. He slumped into a chair across the kitchen table from Stella and studied his hands. "This is a tenant house, Stella. When I was a boy I wouldn't have set foot in a house like this." He bent his head and rubbed the back of his neck with his hands. The hands were scraped and calloused, the nails rimmed with dirt. "Don't you understand? Maggie Grover is offering us everything you've ever dreamed about."

Stella watched the hands. He was saying they could be soft again, that time in the store would ease his shoulders, dry up his sweat, put pounds around his narrow waist.

"I love you, Daddy," she said.

James Earl's fingers relaxed on his neck. "We'll be getting married in October, I guess," he said. "After Anne's baby comes. It'll be a little wedding in Maggie's house, with just Newton and Anne and you children there. Then Maggie and me, we'll go away for a couple of days—that's called a honeymoon."

He grinned because the word embarrassed him. "Then we'll be back living in Maggie's house."

In his words, Stella envisioned the house, now dull in her memory of one Sunday dinner. It had been dark and cool, with heavy furniture that couldn't be moved and dull rugs that couldn't be shook and goblets of such heavy crystal she could barely lift them.

She looked at her father. He was calm now, like a man coming out of anesthesia who realizes he's still alive and can rest easy. Nothing churned in him as it did in her—no secrets crept deeper into his brain— so Stella couldn't tell him what she knew was true.

She wouldn't leave this little house for Maggie Grover's leaden world. She wouldn't set her feet off this land or desert the blood-stained mattress of a grandmother she'd never known. She wouldn't. The brute force of them all combined couldn't make her go. For she knew, as surely as her mother had known the road was home, that this shotgun frame was where her life was. She wouldn't leave it.

Chapter Fifteen

By mid-September James Earl and Maggie Grover were being seen in public. Anne, who had worried at first, put the social considerations as far back in her mind as she could and began thinking how much easier Maggie Grover was making her own situation. She certainly hadn't wanted the responsibility of James Earl's children, especially with her own child to think about. Her baby was going to be special, and even thinking about him now, she would catch herself resenting Lissy, who would continue to play the baby role. Lissy would always be there first.

But now she'd be in Maggie's house three miles away, and they would see James Earl's children on Sundays. Sharing Sunday dinner could turn out to be a good idea, she thought—a social attachment—although she really didn't want Newt and James Earl to lose their renewed family ties. She wanted to love those children, and now she saw the best way to do that was to let Maggie Grover have them.

Of course, there was still the problem of Stella, who said nothing about the marriage and therefore said a lot. Stella was silent only when she was worried. Like when Toby had been so bad off. It had been almost like Stella knew something she couldn't bring herself to say. And when she did say something, she was snappy and irritable, like she was yesterday when Anne finally got some coversation out of her.

They were talking about the baby, but Anne could see Stella's mind drifting off. They were silent for a minute. "What is it, sweetheart?" she asked.

"Oh nothing." Stella turned to look out the nursery window. "I was just thinking about Mama. She shouldn't have had so many babies—some of them died, you know. They were too little to be born. And Lissy, well, she came so quick that Mama bled and bled. I kept scrubbing and wiping, but I just couldn't keep up with it."

"You poor thing," Anne murmured.

"We managed all right." Stella's voice became strident so abruptly that Anne was startled. "We had hard times that I won't ever forget. But we had good times, too. Days when the sky was so pretty and the fields smelled so good. I wanted those days to go on forever because I felt so strong I knew I could work forever.

"And then sometimes we'd have money and could fix the car up or buy something special. Everything we did made me know there was more to do. Just because I never went anywhere important, like fancy restaurants or picture shows or church, that didn't mean I thought I wouldn't ever go. I always, every minute, had hope."

So Stella had exploded at her, and Anne had felt a moment of grief that Stella wasn't her own child. "When you move down to Maggie's, I want you to come back here often," she said. "You can help me with the baby. You'll be special to it, you know. You'll be the baby's cousin."

"I'm not going to Maggie's," Stella said.

"Why, Stella!" Anne put down the baby clothes she'd been folding. "Of course you are. Whatever are you thinking of?"

"I'm going to stay in the little house. Newton will let me. He just has to."

"It isn't Newton's decision to make, Stella. That's for your daddy to decide."

"Well, I'm not going unless you and Newton lock me out. And you wouldn't do that, would you, Anne?"

Stella looked as if she were about to cry, and Anne felt a flood of emotion in herself. But her practical nature ran too deep for her to ignore it.

"But Stella, you can't stay in that house all alone," she protested.

"You and Newton are right here. I can see this house even in the dark. And Toby's just across the field. I won't be alone."

"But Stella, nobody in their right mind would leave a fourteen-year-old girl like that."

"Will Newton make me leave?"

"No, of course not," Anne said hesitantly. "He would never send you away."

"Then I'll stay."

"But why, Stella? When you can live in that wonderful house in town, close to school, where your friends can visit? I bet Maggie's planning on your having a room all your own."

Stella was quiet, searching for words that she knew she could never make Anne truly understand. "You don't know what a house means, Anne," she said finally. "When we were on the road, the six of us in that station wagon, with cars whizzing by or at a filling station or sometimes in one of those diners if

Daddy had a little money, we were so close together. It was a special feeling because we knew it was us against everybody and everything else. There wasn't a place to go where things belonged to us, where we could keep safe a little bit of ourselves. Everything we had went in the car, and all we had was each other. It was such a special thing, like a flower that's just holding onto its petal, because when the petals are gone, the flower will be gone, too. There was nothing holding us together but ourselves.

"But now I have a house with screens on the windows and doors that lock. Even if the wind blows hard, I can be safe in it; and if there's a fire, I can put it out." She stopped, overcome by what she knew she couldn't say.

"But you can have that at Maggie's," Anne argued. "Surely you see that all together in one place you could be happy."

"I can't depend on that," Stella said coldly. "Do you think I can depend on Daddy? Or on Maggie Grover? I don't even know that woman, and here she is telling me everything she's got is mine. That's exactly what she said, and I guess she thinks she means it. But, Anne, that little house is all I really have, and I can't give it up. You'll explain that to Newt, won't you?"

"I'll try, Stella," Anne said finally. "But the truth is I don't understand it myself."

The next time Stella saw Anne, she was in a hospital bed, surrounded by flowers and wearing a lacy bed jacket that Stella had seen her pack but couldn't believe anybody short of a movie star would wear.

Stella had marched down the hall of the hospital

next to Newt, proud that she was fourteen and old enough to come upstairs, while the other children had to sit in the lobby, leafing through ragged magazines. Before they reached Anne's room, Newton took her to the nursery window where the babies were lined up in boxlike beds on rollers, each wrapped in a pink or blue blanket.

"Which one?" Stella asked, and couldn't believe it when Newton didn't know and had to crane his neck to read the cards taped to the bassinets until he found one that read "Willis Boy."

"That's him," Newton said, and Stella laughed out loud because she was so excited and Newton was so foolish.

The baby was sleeping, the side of his face turned to them. His skin seemed tightly stretched, as if there hadn't been enough to cover him, and his hand was a minute fist beside his cheek.

"He's so tiny," Newton whispered, awed by his child's perfection.

Stella was remembering Lissy—hot, slippery, squirming in her trembling hands. Before her eyes flashed the bloody water she'd washed her in, in the same pot that later, when James Earl arrived, held the placenta, which Stella had buried like scraps. Now here was a baby with an announcement at his head, when Stella could remember miscarriages that went unrecorded except in the haunting, fierce memory of birth and death becoming one. He was so clean, the room so bright, the nurse so sterile in her white smock and mask, that Stella wondered how they could have survived at all in the shacks and car, on the edge of dusty fields, with Mae's watery milk their life-food.

They went to see Anne. She was smiling. She

looked and sounded soft, fragile, as precious as the baby, and Stella wanted to kiss her, to touch her purity.

"I talked to Newton and to your daddy," Anne said. "You can stay in the house awhile. Just awhile."

"I'll help you with the baby," Stella said exuberantly. "Every afternoon I can help you."

"And I'll get you a new dress to wear to your daddy's wedding," Anne said. "Jonathan can wear the outfit you picked for him. It will be his first social event, you know."

"We'll all be there," Newton said. "The whole Willis family. You're part of that, Stella."

"You'll let me stay forever, won't you, Newton?" Stella wanted to draw them both close to her.

"We'll see, Stella," he said, but he was smiling. "We have to think about your daddy. He's going to miss you."

"If I'd been in Daddy's place, I'd never have left home," Stella said. "And once I'd come back, I'd never leave again."

The wedding was planned for Saturday afternoon so Maggie and James Earl could be back in town to open the store on Tuesday morning. Maggie had decided to close the store on Saturday afternoon and Monday without even asking James Earl because she wanted to make the momentous decision to be closed any day besides Christmas and Sundays herself. Once they were married, she'd leave the store to him, but until then she would be the proprietress. She really did trust James Earl's decision making, except of course where Stella was concerned. She couldn't believe her ears when he told her he was leaving that child out in that house alone. She knew Newton and Anne were there, and Silas Brown too, but a lot of things could happen to a child, or even to an adult, for that matter.

Besides, Maggie knew more than James Earl did about loneliness, and she'd hoped he'd ask her to talk to Stella. She could tell her about living alone in a house where you heard voices talking in empty rooms just because you wanted to talk to somebody so bad. Sometimes Maggie went to sleep with the television on just for the comfort of the voices. On that little screen there was proof that people could be together.

And aside from the loneliness and danger Stella was subjecting herself to, there were Maggie's feelings to consider. James Earl hadn't seemed to think she should be upset that one of his children wasn't going to be in this house for her to mother. Of course, she knew Stella would be the child to bring her problems if any of them did, although she wasn't really afraid of having a teenager in her charge. Since Stella had abruptly broken off with Rodney Biggers there didn't seem to be a problem with boys—unless Toby Brown was a problem, and she doubted that. Surely Anne would have nipped that one in the bud. Not that Maggie didn't like Toby. He certainly had better manners than most teenagers. She had always welcomed him into her store. But the house. Well, she just didn't know. She had too many other things to think about.

A decorating firm from Lawrence had been upstairs for two weeks working on the empty bedrooms for the children, and she'd told them to decorate a room for a fourteen-year-old girl while they were at it. Outside, the painters were finally working on the trim. Then there was the window washing and some work on the lawn, although the yard seemed to be decorating itself; the maples were bright, the chrysanthemums still in bloom. She had had a new rope put on the swing and decided on a spot near the kitchen window for a sandpile. Alice was cleaning the front parlor and the dining room, but the furnishings were to remain the same. Maggie wanted the rooms to be the way James Earl had first seen them. For herself, she had shopped in Lawrence for new clothes and had bought a smoke blue shantung suit to be married in. She was packing her bag slowly and then daily rearranging it, spreading sachets among her lingerie, fingering the lace and crisp new fabrics.

After the rehearsal on Friday evening, she and James Earl went with Newton and Anne to a restaurant in Lawrence where she ate lobster cocktail and flaming shish-kabob and drank champagne. The next morning, she felt light-headed and woozy even at midday when she locked the store and walked slowly home, knowing that when she got there the house would be empty for the last time. She lounged in the bathtub, hearing Alice below in the kitchen where sandwiches were being arranged on her mother's silver trays. She heard the bakery truck from Lawrence arriving with the cake and the florist with the vases of fresh flowers she'd ordered for the dining room table and the parlor mantel.

Stella was ready long before James Earl, and so she sat on the side porch staring at the sky, almost wishing the flecks of gray autumn clouds would miraculously combine and send a rainstorm down. While she waited, Toby came and sat beside her. She smoothed her skirt. The dress was a rosy color, with a white collar, and smelled new. It reminded her of peach groves.

"That's a new dress," Toby said. "It sure is pretty."

"It's for the wedding. We're all going to the wedding. Then we'll have cake and punch at Maggie's house. Then we're supposed to throw rice at Daddy and Maggie when they get into Newton's car to go off. We'll all come back here until Maggie and Daddy get back Monday afternoon. Then the children will go over there."

"You still staying here?" Toby asked.

"Of course I am." She squinted a little into the sky and tried to suppress the excitement in her voice. "We'll still get on the bus together every morning. And after school we can study together because there won't be Lissy and Earl to take care of."

"I don't know," Toby said slowly. "I've joined the glee club, and I'm thinking I might work on the school paper this year. They need people all the time. I might not be coming home on the bus so much."

"I'll be all right by myself," Stella said. She toyed with her collar.

He could tell he had hurt her. Ever since he'd heard that she planned to stay in the tenant house, he'd been afraid of hurting her, while still wanting to protect himself. He knew she shouldn't depend on him, any more than he could depend on her. And yet, he loved her still, could even fantasize about living in the house with her; an impossible idea he knew, not only because of the Willises and his parents but because loving her was so impossible.

"I think you ought to move into town with your daddy, Stella," he said slowly. "I guess staying out here seems like fun, like acting all grown-up, but it won't be like that. You'll be lonesome. Besides, sooner or later the whole town's going to know about it. The school, too."

"I can tell them I'm staying with Newton and Anne," Stella said. "Nobody needs to know I'm in this house. And I don't think it's one bit fun, Toby. This house belongs to the Willises, and Maggie's house belongs to her. I don't mind Daddy marrying her. I know he needs somebody. But what I need is right here. It's this house and this farm. I wouldn't have left it when I was young the way Daddy did, and I won't leave it now until I see something better to take its place."

"It's just land," Toby argued. "I don't understand what you're expecting from it."

"I expect to take care of myself, Toby, and you can stay late after school every single day if you want to."

"It's time we were going," James Earl said through the screen door. Through the mesh, Stella and Toby could see his new blue suit and white shirt. His face looked ruddy and young as he grinned at them. "This is no time to be late, girl," he said and disappeared to collect the other children.

Stella stood up. "I never owned anything in my life," she said to Toby, "but someday I will, if I don't start letting things slip away right now. I've got to get ahold now. Don't you see that?"

She went down the steps and around the corner toward the car. When she was out of sight, Toby leaned against the porch post and shut his eyes. He could see her still. The vision of her, not just today but every memory he'd saved up, came to him. Stella that first day, standing with Mae before the half-painted house. Stella under the barn shelter handing tobacco, her bra showing through somebody's discarded T-shirt. Stella between himself and Rodney Biggers, and then in his arms after the accident. In his arms again, this time really there with him, aware of him as surely as he had been aware of Rodney Biggers. He would keep on loving her. He just hoped that didn't mean giving up himself.

Anne was playing the old mahogany piano. From the corner of her eye, she could see Maggie reach the bottom of the stairs in her shantung suit. She was carrying the bouquet of orchids the florist had ordered from Raleigh, and her graying hair shone as if she'd put a touch of blueing in it.

She's almost pretty, Anne thought, striking a louder chord of the simplified version of Mendelssohn's "Wedding March."

James Earl was standing in front of the mantel next to the minister, and while looking at Maggie, at how downright good-looking she was when she took the time to fix herself up, he had a flashing memory of Mae. He closed his eyes against it, fighting off the remembrance of her face. He had not loved Mae enough or tried to understand her in the deep, thoughtful way he wanted to know Maggie. Somehow, he could feel confident that Maggie would be with him as long as he lived. She was so stationary. He could moor in her and live quietly, easily, without the rumbling of engines in his head or the cries of children too close to his ears.

Maggie was next to him and she took his arm

heavily, leaning on him because she wanted to give him the sense of oneness she felt. The minister was speaking; she was answering. James Earl was answering, too. She had sat on a church pew through at least a hundred weddings and heard these same words, but until today she'd heard her own loneliness in them. There was no one to love and cherish, no one to stay with her in sickness and health. Never had she been so painfully aware of her own failure as on those occasions when she extended her hand to a bride and groom who were truly oblivious of her.

Anne was playing the piano again. Newton was kissing her cheek. The children were locking around her, even Stella who had always seemed so aloof. James Earl was holding Lissy between them, and Maggie thought how that was as it should be. She kissed the child and then leaned closer to put her face against James Earl's. She'd never touched him in front of people before—even his family—but she didn't feel embarrassment, only a joy that throbbed so intensely she thought she might cry with it.

"Let's have some champagne," she said and drew the children into the dining room with her. "They can have a taste, can't they, James? This is such a special occasion." She heard gaiety in her voice, and she smiled at all of them while Newton opened the bottle and poured the golden bubbles into her mama's crystal goblets. She handed the first glass to Stella. "Wait now," she cried, "until we all have some. Then we'll have a toast, won't we?"

Stella cupped both hands under the bowl of the goblet. Even the stem was cold against her hand. She heard Newton booming a toast, his voice laced with liquor. He stood next to her daddy, with his arm gripping James Earl's shoulder. Her daddy was gulping the champagne and laughing. He didn't seem embarrassed to be standing in Maggie's dining room where the chandelier sparkled and the chairs were heavy with brocade. He seemed right at home.

"To the children," Maggie was saying in a loving tone. She cooed at them, her voice singing. "May they fill this house with laughter."

Stella sipped the champagne. Bubbles flew into her nose. The cold liquid caught fire in her chest. It was delicious. Her family was beautiful, even Maggie, who held Lissy comfortably against the rich fabric of her wedding suit. The gold ring on her finger shone with newness. There were no scratches on it, no dull places. Her daddy wore a ring like it. Stella had never seen him wearing jewelry, and she watched the ring flashing on his lean hand. He is different now, she thought. We are all so different. The champagne was making her light-headed. She wanted to dance, to hold out her peachy skirt and balance herself miraculously on her toes, or sing, or shout, or hug everybody.

"It was a pretty wedding," she said to Maggie. "The prettiest wedding I've ever seen." Her mind wandered forward and backward, flashing the past beside the present. She had never been to a wedding before, had never drunk wine or heard a toast. What had Newton said? "A long and happy life?" Yes, that was it. Was such a thing possible? In her young life, only bad things had lasted long—childbirth, rainy spells, highways. The happy moments had been gone too quickly; spectacles were brief. But perhaps Newton was right. Here there was no rushing, no speed to take her from memory to memory so fast they became blurs. She felt a calm she had never known before. Perhaps her daddy felt it, too. She began to cry. Tears washed down her cheeks.

"Why Stella!" Anne said.

"It's the champagne," Newton advised them. "She's had too much."

They took the empty glass from her hand and sat her down on the parlor sofa. Through the archway she could see the family about the table, tasting, nibbling, drinking, laughing. Watching them, Stella's grief and her joy culminated in one gigantic, tremulous sigh. She would not, she knew, want to change anything.

Chapter Sixteen

There had never been an autumn like this one. The trees held off the coming of winter with their fierce foliage. The dogwoods that edged the pines near Stella's house turned red as blood and stayed there, rimming the dark green depth of the endless forest with a frill of color. The days were still, as the sun moved farther away into a haze of changing seasons. Finally, the wind came to sweep the clouds, turning the pines into giant brooms that brushed endlessly across the sky.

Stella listened from inside her house where she always slept beneath an accumulation of Anne's old blankets in the bed that had belonged to her grandmother. Nightly, she plugged in the electric heater Maggie had given her from the store. Maggie had wanted her to take two, but Stella had refused. The oven in the kitchen would keep that part of the house warm enough, and she had closed off the other rooms from the winter so that she lived in the last bedroom and then scampered down the chilly porch to use the kitchen and bath.

She had lived there alone for only a week when Newton had Silas and Toby up there to board in the side porch. So now her passageway was close and dark. She didn't like it very much because she missed sitting there, where the sky had been so close and the woods so thick and protective. But that wasn't the kind of protection Newton and James Earl thought she needed, so they had built her a wall and latched the screens in tight and put a dead lock on the new door.

They were all keeping her as safe as they could, when what they really wanted was to carry her down to Maggie Grover's house and lock her in a pink, wallpapered room that had white furniture and a bedspread with ruffles down the sides. She'd seen that room, so perfect, so empty of anything human, when she was depositing Lissy in a nursery that looked as fine as Jonathan Willis'. She had stood in the doorway of the room, with Maggie behind her, and felt she must grab hold of the door jamb to keep from being pushed in and the door slammed behind her. The windows were too high for escape; the world would be suddenly, irrevocably, too far outside her reach. But Maggie hadn't pushed her, hadn't even sighed the way Anne did when she wanted to deliver a nonverbal message of chagrin. No, Maggie Grover Willis had been silent, as if she alone understood what little result her voice would have.

Then Stella had wanted to step in. She'd wanted to tell Maggie that the room was truly beautiful and that she was grateful, although she couldn't live there. But those words seemed beyond her, like age itself, and so she turned away from the room and hurried out of the house, because suddenly she could imagine it being her home.

Still, she was glad to be in the little house. Toby had done all the things he'd said he would—joined the choir, worked for the newspaper, had a role in the freshman class play. She got off the bus every morning at the junior high, leaving him to ride on to bigger, better things at the high school. Usually, she didn't see him again until the next morning, when he'd be waiting in front of Newton's house to catch the bus again.

One afternoon after school, she'd gone downtown instead of home, and on the sidewalk outside Maggie's store she'd caught a glimpse of Toby through the reflecting pane. He was coming from behind her, and there was a girl with him—a high-school girl wearing a dress too nice for school and platform shoes. Stella had ducked into the store and leaned against the door as if she'd escaped a hail storm.

"What ails you, girl?" James Earl had said, seeing her panting behind the door, chin tucked in, thick blonde hair still swinging about her face.

"Nothing," she breathed. "I was just running." She felt hot under her sweater, but resisted shedding it. She walked down the aisle past the dry goods and into the shoe department. "Daddy, do you have any shoes with heels on them?"

"Now wouldn't I look foolish walking around like that?" James Earl laughed from his place at the cash register where he could watch the store and the street at the same time. He seemed so much in the center of things now that Stella felt a need to put him a little off balance, to remind him of how she remembered him.

"I mean shoes for me," she pouted, sitting down on one of the two straight-backed chairs in the shoe department. The boxes were all neatly stacked against the wall, with a few shoes sitting on top of them for display. "Everybody's wearing shoes with wedge heels, and here I am in these dumb old loafers."

James Earl left the cash register and sat down on the fitting stool in front of her. "Now I know what seventh-grade folks are wearing. Don't I sell it to 'em?"

"No, you don't," Stella said, "because the girls I know go to Lawrence shopping. They say Maggie's clothes came off the ark."

She expected him to be angry, but he was smiling. "Well, hellfire, they ain't far from wrong. Just this morning a salesman was by here with blouses for ladies and girls. Here he comes with these things that button up the front. So I say to him, "Where's the pullover kind? Those turtle-necks, and ones without a collar at all. That's what folks are wearing." Well, I can tell you he was surprised. Maggie'd been buying the same blouses for the last ten years. So I did some ordering, not spending any more than she does, but getting something girls like you will be wanting."

She could see the excitement in his face. Like a child discovering he can ride a bicycle, her daddy had discovered he could buy and sell. She could see it pleased him.

"Well," she said, "when you get those chunky-heeled shoes, you let me know."

"Yes, ma'am. I sure will do that." James Earl slapped his knees.

"How about you hanging around here and eating supper with us. Maggie's home with the children already, and Alice is frying chicken."

Generally Stella found a way of avoiding going to Maggie's. She didn't like to sit in the big old kitchen where the light was bright and the food smelled so good her stomach jumped and churned through the prayers. But outside, the afternoon waned, the wind took on a chilly look, and she didn't really want to go home and eat Anne's leftover soup. "All right," she said finally. "If you don't mind taking me home."

"I wish you'd stay with us, Stella," James Earl said. "You've got a room right there waiting."

"I know, Daddy, but not yet. I can't come yet."

"Well," he said, getting up. "You can help me close up this place. It'll be five o'clock before we know it. Maggie wants us to bring ice cream home, too." He was adjusting shades in the display window.

Stella unfolded the white cover sheets over the bolts of cloth. The store became eery, the oiled floorboards creaked, and wind shook the window-panes softly.

"You just got that sweater?" James Earl asked, slipping into a new plaid jacket. "You better be wearing your coat these days. It could snow anytime now. Temperature drops every night, and there're rings around the moon."

"Oh, Daddy." Stella clutched her books while he turned out the lights.

The long aisles of the store changed form in the shadows, were no longer straight and orderly, but floating in their gowns like long, drifting ghosts.

When they arrived at the house, there was a fire laid on the parlor hearth, and even before calling to Maggie and the children, James Earl stopped to light it. Stella could see the fire lighting had already become a ritual of the late autumn nights. She could see that there were bonds growing between Maggie and her daddy that showed themselves in the lighting of fires at twilight; the silent bowing of heads at the table; the way he hoisted Lissy onto his shoulders to take her up to bed; the expression on Maggie's face when he swung the baby under the hall chandelier; her relaxed smile when Lissy was safe in his arms again.

"Well, hello," Maggie said to them from the parlor door. "I smelled the fire." She came into the room and rested her hands on James Earl's chest for a moment. "Stella, how wonderful to have you! The children miss you, you know. We all do."

Stella could feel the aura of love, the smell of smoke, the warmth of the fire mingling around her. "Daddy asked me to stay for supper," she said.

"We're having chicken, too," Maggie said. "I sometimes think Alice gets secret messages from you. But look here, that ice cream's melting. Take it into the kitchen, dear, and I'll get the children washed up."

Stella held the cold sack against her sweater. The hallway seemed shorter than before, not a shadowy passageway but a lived-in place with light to illuminate both the way and the framed photographs that spoke of Maggie's past.

In just minutes, they would all be around Maggie's table. She would be looking at the children, who seemed already to have forgotten the fields and shacks, the battered station wagon. William probably never said a word when he saw that new car in the garage, probably never asked what happened to the station wagon or the shacks or his mother. He was already forgetting, and that was just as well. Not everybody is supposed to remember, Stella thought. Just some of us. Someday I guess I'll understand why that is.

After supper, Stella got into the new car James Earl had bought with Maggie's money, and they whizzed down the street and out of town while the car heater purred at her cold legs.

"I don't want to see you downtown without a coat again," James Earl said. "You ain't used to this kind of weather. I'm telling you, Stella, we'll have a snow before December's out. By Christmas."

"I promise to wear a coat," Stella said to silence him. The night moved around her. They left the street lights behind, and the car was dark and warm. Stella tried to think which way the car was taking her—forward or backward. Back to the farm, she decided finally. Back where I belong. Then Maggie's house must be forward. Could it be that they were all moving forward but her?

"Daddy, tell me about Grandmother Willis."

"There ain't much to tell, I don't reckon. Mama was one of those people folks like, but there isn't a lot she did or said you could remember or tell about. What I remember best are things I can't describe, like the way her apple cobbler tasted or the sound she made when she laughed. She didn't laugh much, but when she did, it was a sound that was just longing to get out. Sometimes you sound like her—both when you're laughing and when you're mad. Mama had a temper, but she held onto it better than you do."

"When she killed herself, was she mad then?"

"Maybe she was, in a way. She was tired, more than anything. The sickness she had gave her a lot of pain, and she knew she'd never get better. In a way, she was being stubborn, the way you can be, Stella. She died her way, not somebody else's." He turned the car up the path and the lights beamed on Stella's house. "I guess you're living your way and not anybody else's," he said. "I admit it hurts me. I worry about you, and I miss having you with me. I always thought we got along pretty good together."

"We did, Daddy. We still do." Stella eased the door open. Cold air swept against her legs. "I'm glad you're happy. I'm glad for all of us." She raced toward the house, with a black shadow of herself moving in the headlights.

When the car had pulled away, she turned on the heater and sat in the dark of her bedroom, feeling the chill leaving the room. The orange glow of the electric coils played in the air, warming her. She didn't want to go to bed, so after awhile she got up and put on the coat her daddy had demanded she wear.

She couldn't remember a night as cold as this one. The moon was very bright, and the two houses closest to her seemed very near. Both of them were dark, like shadows set into hedges and shrubbery. Outside, she walked down the field toward Toby's house. He was there asleep, dreaming maybe about the girl in the expensive dress or about college or even some of the little dreams he'd told her about. But he was outside her reach now. She had put him there by some now strange, almost foreign idea that he was not as good as she was.

She stood in the field hoping a light would come on, hoping Toby would know she had come. But there was nothing but the night around her, the moon moving, the wind stirring in the pines.

Back in her little house, she turned off the heater and climbed into bed. At first she thought she wouldn't sleep. Her mind spun the memory of the dinner at Maggie's, twisting it, lighting it with firelight, looping it over and over in a knot that wouldn't turn her loose. They were happy. All of them. Maybe she should go to live in town. She could try it for awhile, as long as she knew she could come back to the farm whenever she wanted to. Maybe Toby would walk her home sometimes and come into the kitchen. She wanted him to see how big that kitchen was and how her room looked and how the chandeliers glittered, not to brag about them but to share them with him.

But maybe that couldn't be. There was an overpowering sense of past in Maggie's house that would awe Toby just as it awed her. Yet the house attracted her too, sent a spark of longing deep inside to make her stomach quiver uneasily with delight and expectation at the rich food smells, the colored soaps, the soft towel she'd rubbed against Lissy's cheek, the family portraits in the hall.

Still, if she were to move there, it would have to be a house Toby could come to. It would have to be a place where she belonged.

Chapter Seventeen

Rodney Biggers sat on a stool in the soda shop watching Toby Brown out of the corner of his eye. The kids in the gang Toby was hanging out with were all freshmen from high school, but they were kids from good families. Rodney wished he knew why in high school, where everything was so difficult for him, Toby Brown had gotten popular.

Now he watched the girl next to Toby lean closer to him in the booth, as if she intended to whisper something to him. But she didn't. They just looked at each other and started smiling like they were someplace else and the jukebox wasn't blinking its colored lights and Elsie wasn't fussing over cola spilled on the floor.

"This ain't your kitchen at home," one of the kids was saying to Elsie, and she, slapping the wet string mop to the floor tiles, glared up at him. "And it ain't your pigpen either."

The kids laughed, and Rodney felt sudden empathy with Elsie, who seemed thwarted in her effort to do her dreary job halfway right. After all, Rodney hadn't wanted anything but Stella Willis, a girl in junior high school, a foreigner in the town. He hadn't set his eye on a high-school girl, much less a town girl. Stella suited him fine. But somehow his one great effort to keep her had backfired on him and given Toby Brown a mysterious new start. Rodney felt sure the "accident" had resulted in Toby being able to abandon himself to whatever life offered him. Now he seemed willing to take his chances with people; a risk Rodney felt he'd never be equipped to take.

"Whatcha know, Rodney?" someone was saying.

Rodney looked up to find Toby standing next to him. "What do you want?" he blurted.

"Nothing, man. Just speaking to you." The kids from the booth were ganging around them. Some of them leaned against the counter behind Rodney.

"You all get away from here," Elsie yelled. "How can I wait on the paying customers with you monkeys hanging onto the counter like that?"

"Come on and take a ride with us," Toby said to Rodney. "Charlene here, she's got her daddy's car and a full tank of gas."

Charlene took hold of Toby's arm. "He doesn't want to come. He's still mooning around over that little Willis girl, aren't you, Rodney? Used to be driving her around everywhere you looked, but she got smart, I reckon. Or was she too old for you, Rodney. Fourteen's mighty old."

"Shut up about Stella," Toby commanded. "She's not in this, Charlene. You wanta come, Rodney?"

"No," Rodney gasped. "I got to get over to the shop in a minute."

The other kids laughed and began drifting toward the door.

"I guess you got reason to be scared of me," Toby said before he moved away.

Oh Lord, he was going to start bawling right there

in the soda shop. Rodney faked a sneeze and wiped his eyes and face with his handkerchief.

"You're coming down with something," Elsie accused. "Why don't you go on home."

Rodney slid off the stool. "You remember a couple of months ago somebody beat up Toby Brown? Well, I know who did it."

"Shut your mouth, boy," Elsie said, already wiping the countertop where he'd been. "I don't want to hear that kind of rot."

So nobody wanted to know. Already the incident was buried, locked deep like the scars on Toby Brown's ribs. Maybe even Toby was forgetting, maybe even Stella was. Rodney felt the tears stinging. He would be the one to remember. Only he. Alone.

The week after Thanksgiving, when the cold had settled on the countryside in brown patches of frosty grass and the windows of the little house were icy and rattling with winter wind, Stella left school during the lunch break and walked slowly to Maggie's, taking a long, chilling, inconspicuous route that made her arrive at the kitchen door just after James Earl had returned to the store.

Alice was in the kitchen, the dishwater steaming into her glistening face, and she hardly seemed surprised at Stella's shivering form in the doorway. "Miss Maggie's putting Lissy to bed," she whispered. "You go on up there if you want to. Just tread soft."

Stella dropped her coat on a chair and slipped down the hall. She could hear Maggie singing. Her voice warbled slightly, unsure of the melody, like a child learning a new tune, but a haunting quality in the husky sound made Stella pause on the stair and listen intently, her fingers gripping the banister tightly as she strained her ears over the slosh of kitchen water and the humming wind outside. The voice was mournful and struggled on the notes. The words were undistinguishable. Soft *s*'s hung in the air, and rising with them was a sound that caught Stella's ear so purely that she felt tears springing to her eyes; she knew she was hearing the sound of love. Never had she heard it so clearly before, not in textbook poems or in love scenes on flickering movie screens, not even in her daddy's voice when it came to her across the muffled sound of babies breathing in the night. It was music—richly, harmoniously, undeniably true.

"Maggie," she whispered at the half-closed door. There was a moment of silence, and then the song continued softly, moving across the room toward her. The door opened slightly, and she saw Maggie smile and then pause in her song again to put her finger across her lips.

Maggie eased through the slit in the doorway and drew Stella silently into the next room, which Stella realized, with a sudden tingling gasp, was the pink and ruffled place Maggie had created for her.

"She's asleep," Maggie said in a whisper. "She usually goes right off without a fuss, but today little Earl is spending the afternoon with a nursery-school friend and she misses him." She paused and let go of Stella's hand. "Sometimes I think they miss more than we realize. It's so easy to forget that their worlds are very small, and so every single thing is so important to them. I mean, sometimes I forget that I'm not really their mother, that they remember someone else . . ." She paused again and stared at

Stella as if she'd just realized who she was speaking to.

"Oh, Stella," she said quickly. "Whatever is the matter? It's too early for school to be out."

"I got a sick pass," Stella said. "Mrs. Daley is very sympathetic about cramps." She smiled a little, feeling good that she could tell Maggie the truth.

"You pretended?" Maggie tried to look displeased.

"Yes, I wanted to see you." Stella sighed and looked at the room. "This is so pretty," she said. "It's almost too pretty, you know. If somebody really lived here, they might mess it up."

"Oh, no," Maggie said. "What it needs is somebody living in it. This room has always been needing you, Stella."

Stella sat down gingerly on the bed, while Maggie fingered the china statue of a colonial lady that decorated the base of the dresser lamp.

"I came to tell you something, Maggie." She paused and shuddered in the silent room, believing she must control all her courage, direct it carefully into the words she wanted to say. "I've been thinking about this ever since Daddy married you and I wouldn't come here with him after you fixed up this room, and Daddy had begged me and I knew you were hurt about it. I didn't really want you to be hurt, Maggie, but somehow I felt good about it, too. I knew it meant you cared about what happened to me—to all of us.

"But, you see, at first I saw what belonged to you as yours—just yours—and I couldn't see you sharing it with us. I couldn't trust your giving us things. I didn't think you cared about us that much. Loving never seemed to have anything to do with giving before. Daddy and Mama never had anything to give. None of us ever owned anything until we came back to Daddy's home and Newton gave us that little house. But, somehow, I felt like it had always been ours. That land out there belonged to us no matter what anyone said. Daddy was born to it, and I was born to Daddy; so the land and the house were mine. They truly belonged to me, and I belonged to them, like I had known the house and land long before and had somehow forgotten about them for a while."

She stopped and looked at Maggie, who leaned against the wall, surrounded by the pink and glowing wallpaper, her arms across her stomach, her head bent forward slightly. She was looking straight at Stella and listening.

"I love it so much, Maggie. I thought nobody could understand but me, and so I've never tried very hard to say it. But now I know I hurt you and Daddy by staying in the only place I felt I belonged. I could have tried to say it like I'm trying now.

"But somehow, lately, I've been thinking you'd understand because your house and the store—the things you've been giving Daddy and all of us—belonged to you even before you were born. It's like a root deep in the ground. You can't see it, but you know it's there, because the tree is there. So I came to tell you that I'm sorry I couldn't leave my place and come here, and I want to say that I think I will someday. Sometime, maybe soon, I think I can leave my little house and not be giving it up, because what I feel about it will come with me."

She didn't know when she had begun crying, but

suddenly the pink room was a blur and Maggie's arms were around her, steadying her trembling shoulders.

"I can love you, Stella," Maggie said softly. "And I know about holding on to what belongs to you. That was all I knew until I found your daddy. Then I learned there were better things than being brave and pretending to like a life that's hard and lonely. It's not always easier to love people more than things, but I've learned it's worth the risk." She smoothed Stella's dry hair with her hand and then straightened her up so that they faced each other. "You must be tired out, walking all the way from school on a windy day like this. I bet you skipped lunch, too, didn't you?"

Stella nodded, unable to speak.

"Then you lie down right here on this bed, and I'll go down and get you some hot chocolate and a sandwich. I think I'll have something myself." She smiled and patted Stella's hand. "You don't have to be afraid of this room," she said gently. "Remember, it's just a place, and places don't really own people, do they?"

The autumn sun was golden in the room. Silence swept down the hall at Maggie's feet and left only the slight hush of leaves against the window. The bed was soft, the covers deep and boundless. Stella felt her body warming them, seeping through her jeans and shirt into the new cloth of the sheets. I can't stay, she thought, but her eyes were closing. Not yet. I can't.

When she awoke an hour later, the room was still rosy, hazy with midafternoon, but it didn't look the same to her. There was no threat in it; no demon to capture her separateness and make her one with Maggie Grover's world if she didn't choose to be. There was still the farm and the woods and the house beyond, and before that afternoon waned into twilight, she went back to it.

The Sunday after the new year began, Stella awoke early. She had her suitcase packed and a box of paraphernalia she'd accumulated while living alone carefully taped shut by the door, ready to be carried away with her. But what had awoken her so suddenly wasn't the excitement and dread of moving to Maggie's house, but a brightness in her room that was too white and glaring for sunlight alone.

Even before she reached the window, she knew what it must be. The field beside the house was covered with snow. She raced to the other window and looked out at the woods. The trees were gloriously frosted.

She dressed quickly and went out on the wide porch and into the yard, where she buried her gloveless hands in the pockets of her coat and pulled her shoulders up against the breathtaking cold. The snow still fell lightly, as if it were finishing the lace on a gigantic white spread. Flakes touched her hair and coat, but melted almost before she could see them.

"Stella!" Anne called from her back porch. "Come get these mittens!"

"I'm all right!" she answered. "I'm not cold!"

Toby was jumping the gulleys in the field. "I was coming to wake you up," he called breathlessly.

"I think I felt it in my sleep," Stella said when he reached her. "I just knew this had to be a special day.

I'm going to town, you know. Anne and Newt are taking me to Daddy and Maggie's for dinner, and I'm staying."

"Yeah." Toby kicked into the snow and studied the white powder in the air. "I'm going to miss you."

"You'll come to see me, won't you, Toby? I want you to."

"Sure, I'll be around."

"I mean it, Toby. I couldn't stand it if I thought you wouldn't come."

"I'll come," Toby said. "I promise."

He was already gone when Newton came out and called to Stella and she carried her belongings over to the car and shut them in the trunk. The little house looked so empty from where she stood beside the car, although she knew the furniture from the attic was still there—the fearful mattress, the dishes and linens they'd used. And yet, Stella knew the house had long been empty, so when she was snug in the car beside her uncle and they were turning away toward the highway and the town, she didn't look back, not out of any trembling emotion, but because she knew where the future was.

The town came to them slowly, one house at a time, until suddenly, almost without warning Stella felt, they were before the ancient house, where smoke and light and snow mingled like the magic of life itself. "Well," she said to Anne and Newt, "we're here."

Then the door was flung open and, as the house's warmth slammed into her with arms and legs and milky breath, she could hear the house itself saying, "We're here."

Sue Ellen Bridgers was born and raised in North Carolina, in the heart of the country she describes so movingly in *Home Before Dark*. She attended East Carolina University and was recently graduated from Western Carolina University. Her stories and articles have appeared in *Redbook, Ingenue,* and *The Carolina Quarterly.*

Sue Ellen Bridgers, her husband, and their three children now live in Sylva, North Carolina. This is her first novel.